'A moving coming of age novel ... Between its political intrigues and emotional highs and lows, *A Dragonfly's Wing* sheds light on underwritten issues.'
– Indies Today

'Hard-hitting prose enhances this potent narrative in a seemingly effortless depiction of real life.'
– The BookLife Prize

'An astounding work of contemporary fiction ... written with great empathy and keen observation.' – SPR

'Donato does not shy away from the raw and powerfully emotive truths ... a highly recommended read for fans of deep personal dramas and social commentary in fiction.'
– K.C. Finn, Readers' Favorite

'He is becoming an icon to the LGBT community.'
– Stephanie Cirami, IAOTP

'A man who exemplifies what it means to reinvent yourself ... Jeremy [writes] about the power of choice and the impact of culture, class and socioeconomic status.'
– Breakaway Daily

Self-Portrait with Cigarette
Edvard Munch, 1895

A Dragonfly's Wing

JEREMY C BRADLEY-SILVERIO DONATO

Eiffel Tower Press
Paris | London | New York
www.eiffeltowerpress.com

Cover photography © iStock/Getty Images

The characters in this book are fictitious and any resemblance to real persons, living or dead, is purely coincidental.

A Dragonfly's Wing / Bradley-Silverio Donato. —1st ed.

Hardcover EAN 2370000778727
Paperback ISBN 978-1-7332603-3-6
E-book ISBN 978-1-7332603-4-3

A note on the usage of foreign words: Where they are rendered in the original language, words and phrases are in *italics* and capitalised according to the conventions of the language. Where these words are rendered in English, they are styled according to the standard grammar conventions. For example, schnitzel is written thusly in English but as *Schnitzel* in German.

For Larry,
who was my biggest cheerleader.

And for Rayetta,
who never got to see it happen.

Being no more than a man,
you cannot tell what tomorrow will bring,

Nor how long one who appears blessed
will remain that way.

The overturning of a dragonfly's wing
is not more swift than the fate of man.

Simonides of Ceos

Prologue

It wasn't until chicken schnitzel and Sacher torte that Jon Evans began to realise the full consequences of his actions. The Frenchman had been dead for several weeks by then.

Their meeting was fortuitous, he remembered, though not as unlikely nor as preordained as he would have liked to believe.

It was a Saturday morning, and Jasmine had just stepped up to the podium to deliver her speech. It was Jon's speech, he reminded himself. He had written it. But no one would know. Her fluent delivery and the scant usage she made of the teleprompter ensured that all eyes were on the new prime minister. All eyes except her husband Jon's, who was glaring at the young man two rows away.

'Thank you, thank you, thank you.' As she repeated the phrase, each time her voice box reached the long 'u' syllable, the crowd grew quieter, until at last only the shuffle of feet could be heard.

The man, mid-thirties, had sweeping brown hair that thinned at the temples and a cropped beard that hinted at some exotic origin. The beard's hairs were a shade darker than the hair on his head, and they bent at the ends almost to a curl. His blue eyes were piercing, and although he looked at Jasmine, or rather at the back of her head, Jon felt that the man's eyes were also looking at him sideways, everywhere and nowhere at the same time.

Jasmine was on the fifth or sixth sentence now. She paused. The audience cheered on cue.

Jon looked down at the cardboard programme and found the man's name on the attendees list. Jean-Pierre Mokrani, cultural attaché of France.

Mokrani was a regular on the cable news circuit before his appointment to the embassy. Jon and Jasmine had lived in Paris then. France 24, Al Jazeera, CNN, Euronews, TV5Monde. Mokrani was always on one of these channels, engaged in a panel on a contemporary cultural issue or answering questions about his party's latest political move in opposition to the government. It had been a shock when this rising star on the sociopolitical scene accepted the French president's request to join the foreign service, quashing his ability to speak openly and critically. The media had even suggested that the French government had coaxed him into service in a keeping-your-enemies-closer strategy. In short, this was precisely the man Jon needed.

Mokrani shifted his gaze in Jon's direction. But only for a moment. Then he was staring at the back of Jasmine's head again. But in that moment, they were entirely the same, Jon Evans and Jean-Pierre Mokrani, in their ridiculous roles, warming the benches in crumpled morning suits, with wandering eyes and tight lips.

Part One

'Every moment happens twice: inside and outside,
and they are two different histories.'

Zadie Smith

ONE

I.

Milo first appeared in New Bond Street on 21 March, the first day of spring. Tereza, his mother, and Arsenije, her most recent boyfriend, sent Milo there with a faded tartan blanket, three pounds sterling in coins, a felt top hat, and a crude cardboard sign. The instructions were clear: place the blanket in a visible, high-traffic area, and sit down. Position the hat in front of you, and prop the cardboard sign in front of the hat. Place the coins in the hat. Look sad. And wait.

II.

Terence stepped out of the Green Street tube station at 9:30 a.m. This was an early morning for him, but he'd had a hard time sleeping, tossing in his plump, feather-filled bed until about three and then waking up before eight. The tossing-about annoyed him more than the sleeplessness did. The designer bed had cost more than a few months' salary—a true luxury to someone whose income could vary from month to month as drastically as his did—and for what? Only to toss about in discomfort. Had honesty prevailed, Terence would have admitted to himself that his overworked mind, not the pricey bed, was the real culprit. But staggering across the busy London thoroughfare, his thoughts were on caffeine, not philosophy or psychiatry. The city buzzed this time of morning, and the long line outside his usual Starbucks surprised Terence; he was used to being one of only a handful of people there at his usual 10:45 arrival time. The urge for a caffeine jolt was stronger than his patience to queue or any brand loyalty, so Terence did what anyone with a mild stimulant addiction running on five hours of sleep would do: he went to find the next nearest café.

III.

Although New Bond Street was a change of scenery, a new workplace so to speak, Milo had no problem setting up his station. And why would he? They had given him the same instructions the last time (at an intersection in Piccadilly Circus) and before that too (on the high road of a Leicestershire village). Only minor details were ever altered: the show money would increase or decrease based on Arsenije's analysis of how much would appear reasonable to passersby. Tereza and Arsen might ask Milo to dress differently, sometimes in tatty hand-me-downs, sometimes disguised as a backpacker or a down-on-his-luck ne'er-do-well. But today, he'd been told to rely on the tried and tested homeless trope. That meant jeans with holes in them like tears from a giant mouse's gnawing, trainers without laces and socks, and an oversized T-shirt. He had attempted to explain to his mother and to Arsen that holey denim, no-show socks, and oversized T-shirts were trendy these days, but they couldn't grasp the concept.

'You're just trying to get out of going again,' Tereza said.

'You gotta believe me. It's normal to dress like this now.'

'Nevertheless,' Arsenije replied in his accented English so that it sounded like *nay-vay-duh-less*, 'You're going!' And with that, they put Milo on the bus outside their temporary dwelling at a hostel in Croydon. He got off an hour later in New Bond Street, accoutrements in tow.

IV.

Two doors from his usual Starbucks, Terence entered a no-brand café. A sign with the single word 'Coffee' hung over a wooden door. Only the tiniest amount of sunlight crept into the shop from a single pane of glass. There was no queue, though, and only one customer inside, an old man in his late seventies, perhaps a leftover fixture of the neighbourhood's once-thriving Old Masters art scene or perhaps just a doorman at one of the grand old hotels nearby getting his Americano before his shift began. Terence's spirits lifted. In three off-and-on years of patronising the Starbucks, he had never ventured a mere two doors down. But wait, was there something wrong with this place? Why would people wait on line for five, ten, or even fifteen minutes for a coffee so mass-produced that it had the same taste no matter where they were in the world, when they could get a better variety just a few feet down the road? Yes, there had to be something wrong with this no-name, no-customer place.

'Can I help you?'

Shit. The yellow-eyed, middle-aged store assistant had snuck up from behind the café's pinewood serving counter. *Well, what difference did it make now?* Terence thought. Any coffee would do, even this one.

'Double mocha.'

'A pound-fifty, please.'

'For a double? That's it?'

The assistant, whose name tag he now noticed read 'James,' nodded his head and smiled. Terence pulled out his bank card, involuntarily moving it in a downwards motion as though he were paying using the contactless feature.

'Oh, sorry,' said James, 'cash only.' He pointed to a handwritten sign on the door's window.

Terence froze, then began desperately patting the sides of his trouser pockets. Nothing there. He searched the pockets of his rucksack. Nothing there either save a few paper receipts and an old electric bill.

'I, uh, I need...' What would he do? Go to the cashpoint? Fine, fine, but that would take the same amount of time as if he had waited in the queue at Starbucks. Damn it!

'Don't sweat it,' said James. 'This one is on the house.'

'Are you certain?' Terence couldn't bring himself to look at James, this sunray-haired, chubby shop assistant. Eye contact would make it too real. Though it was a small gift of only a pound and a half, probably nothing of real value to the store's inventory, it had saved Terence from a minor humiliation. He looked away for a moment, then bit his lower lip and looked up at James, grateful for the kindness of a stranger.

James smiled again, and pushed the Styrofoam cup across the counter.

V.

By 10:00, the suits and brogues and high-heels had disappeared into office buildings and storefronts. Sharp tourists and chic locals replaced them, wearing faded denim cutoffs, sneakers, and white T-shirts. But Arsen had been right on some level: you could distinguish these folks by their designer bags, by the brand labels on their shoes, and the Rolex watches on their wrists.

There was a trick to working the streets, and there was a goal. The trick was to look ahead, or down, or up, or across… at a vantage point so remote that it was clear you were not sleeping or otherwise preoccupied (from intoxication, for example) but that you held on to some decency, some self-respect. You did not look your patrons in the eye. Milo had tried that before, and his glare had outed him. The goal, then, was twenty quid per day. It had been £15, but Tereza became unconvinced that she could feed herself and, at the same time, enable Arsen's various gambling, drinking, and smoking habits on a mere £450 per month. Twenty quid per day, and Milo could keep two. He thought, more than a few times, of holding onto the excess on days when the felt top hat came in over budget. But skimming more than his share seemed fraught with problems, not the least of which was what would happen to him if they found out. It had been enough that once he'd had a cheeseburger and fries. When Tereza found the crumpled receipt in the pocket of that week's chino uniform, she'd yelled at him for five minutes. But the whipping from Arsen's imitation leather belt had left deep purple and magenta scars that still hurt if Milo thought too long about them. And if he thought about those scars, he thought about the other ones, too. The scars no one could see, the scars that would only manifest if he let his mind reach far back. Today, he fixed his vantage point on a crowded Starbucks on the opposite corner. The constant flow of people moving in and out made for interesting people watching and kept his mind off remembering. It was working, too. More than a dozen people had crossed the streets on their way to wherever they were going and dropped some coins into his top hat, seeming remnants of their caffeine-addicted payments. Just judging from the amount of foot traffic, Milo estimated he was at nine or ten pounds already. Every half hour, he'd glance around to ensure no one was looking and then swoop out the bulk of the money, transferring it to his pocket, leaving a little show money. When most of the day labourers moved inside, though, traffic slowed. Even the Starbucks was empty. Two doors down, a shop with only the word 'Coffee' above its entryway held even less appeal. Milo sighed. He knew there was little use in complaining. There were worse things, he imagined, like sleeping in a park. And two pounds a day was enough to get a sandwich if someone didn't offer him food, which they normally did. With the roughly £300 he'd saved already, he might get away soon, maybe fly to the States or take a train north, look for work, maybe go to school, and afford a simple room somewhere. Just a little while longer, and the money in the small wooden matchbox he kept in his rucksack would pave the way to something better. Just as long as Arsen didn't get wind of it. Milo felt sure his

mother's boyfriend would not take kindly to a hidden
stash of small notes.

VI.

By 11:30, Terence needed a break. He had sat in
one of Coffee's faux-marble-topped tables, nursing the
double mocha for far too long, and besides, he could
do with some fresh air to recover his thoughts.

He began gathering his things. 'Hey, thanks for the
drink.'

'No problem,' said James, flashing another of his
eager smiles. 'Hope we'll see you again.'

'I'm sure you will,' said Terence, and meant it. He'd
thought more clearly and wrote more lucidly here than
he'd done in weeks at the commercial chain.

Outside, New Bond Street was now as he knew it:
tree-lined, bright, and calm. Though the tube station
was located around the corner to the left past Starbucks, Coffee had been such a happy bit of luck born
of desperation that Terence turned right, intending to
see what the other end of Bond Street might hold.
Sure, he'd been there on the odd shopping or dining
excursion, but he'd not really *been* there, not seen past
its glitzy storefronts and tuxedoed doormen.

But already there was trouble. As Terence crossed the road heading north, his left foot stumbled behind his right, causing him to skip in an awkward two-step, like an unrehearsed Ginger Rogers. He turned to look back. Christ, a beggar. He'd tripped over the beggar's, what was it? Hat. His hat. And now a stream of coins splayed at right angles along the pavement. Well, he'd have to go back and help the boy pick up the money. Yes, he could see now it was a boy, not your typical beggar. But then, Terrence would have to leave something, and he had nothing to give, no change, no bills. Beggars didn't take credit cards any more than indie coffee shops did. And really, it *was* the boy's fault. This was a pedestrian zone. Did his paraphernalia really need to be in the way of people who were minding their own business? People who worked and made their own living. Terence moved his right foot and then his left and strode up Bond Street, holding his head high.

VII.

Milo grew increasingly distracted on the bus ride home that evening. This was supposed to be his time to decompress, to read, and to be as normal as his life allowed. Reading was the one luxury he was afforded and his only schooling. Every tiny noise, every shuffle of the other passengers on and off irritated him, until, at last, he closed the book, flipping it around to look at the back cover. Many of the books Milo read were ugly, torn things, fished from rubbish bins or snatched from recently unoccupied seats of unfortunate commuters who'd left their travel reading material behind. But his current read, which he'd farmed with painstaking precision out of the crevices between two double-decker bus seats last week, appeared almost new. The binding was firm and without crease; the paperback covers retained the gentle shine of fresh ink. *Noon at the Louvre,* a novel by Terrence O. Matthews. Milo was only a quarter of the way in, but the blurb on the back rang true. (Normally, he never bothered reading *about* a book before reading the book. That was a luxury reserved for people who have a choice in what they read.) This was the story of a politician who finds herself wrapped up in a scandalous Parisian affair, told from the viewpoint of her husband. In bold print on the top of the back cover, a blurb from a popular newspaper said: 'With echoes of recent British scandal, one wonders just how much of this is make believe.' Perhaps not the kind of book Milo would pick up given the choice, but the escapism was divine. For maybe an hour a day to and from, all his own. He would sometimes pray for the bus to run behind schedule or for the traffic to delay the journey. Not that there was a god to pray to. Still, prayer couldn't hurt.

But there was no relief, not today. No answer to his invocations. Stepping through the half-dilapidated, sheet metal door of their hostel room, Milo immediately emptied his pockets of the £25.50 in assorted bills and coins and then at once handed his rucksack to Arsen for inspection.

'What's this?' the man asked, turning the bag upside down to ensure Milo had hidden no coins in its crannies. He held the almost-new book in his grimy, browning hands.

'A book.' Milo's instinct was to grab it from Arsen's hands. But remembering the belt, he thought better.

'I can see that, obviously.' This came out as *ob-vay-us-lee*. 'Where did you get it?'

'Same place I always do. From the rubbish bin.' Not entirely true but close enough.

'Good. So long as you spend no money.'

'Don't have any to spend.' Milo reached for the bag and stuffed the book along with his other belongings back into it. The sweat from his palms rubbed off on the novel's cover. If they ever dug around in the bag... found the matchbook hidden in the interior compartment with the broken zipper...

'Don't get smart with your father.' Since lifting her head from the usual evening chore of counting the day's haul and then depositing it into the glass jar she kept near her pillow, the first words Tereza spoke were spiked with vitriol.

Milo knew better than to say the words he wanted to —*He's not my father*—so he tried to lighten the mood. 'Yeah, well, it was a good one. Exceeded the goal.'

'Yeah,' she said, 'that's true. Here's your two quid.' She threw at him an assortment of five, ten, and twenty-pence pieces so that the volume hid the truth of the worth. It was always like this. Tereza preferred to keep the larger denominations for herself and Arsen-ije. It made no difference to Milo. He'd long ago stopped being ashamed of using change to pay for things, and what he didn't spend on food or toothpaste or deodorant, he exchanged for paper bills at one of those automatic teller machines often found in the lob-bies of big-box stores, afterwards transferring the cash to his covert matchbox.

That matchbox had become his private bank, his medium-to-long-term savings plan, and the receptacle for all the dreams that secondhand books could not hold. With any luck or any reprieve from the god he didn't believe in, he would add those two pounds to his bank on the next morning's bus journey, out of the sight of his 'parents.'

Outside the barred windows of the ground floor hostel room, the sound of mosquitos rang high as the sky gave up its blueness for the warmth of a pink and orange summer night. Milo looked down at the timepiece on his left wrist, a black, plastic band fitted with a grey-toned face flashing 21:04. The watch was the nicest thing he owned, the only real thing he could claim for himself, a holdover from happier—or if not happier, at least less complicated, less dire—times. The small chromium battery would run out any day now, he knew, and then he'd have to withdraw something from his private cardboard banker. A watch was no good without its battery. So, it would be worth paying a part of his savings to have something of value, however minuscule, to continue calling his own.

'What's for dinner?' he asked, turning again to Tereza.

She sighed. 'Your father and I have eaten—'

'But... what...' Milo's throat tightened. She could be curt, inconsiderate, but rarely this heartless. At least he'd always been able to count on Tereza for dinner—macaroni and cheese, a ham sandwich, beans on toast—or something approximating dinner. 'I don't understand why you'd eat without—'.

'Keep your voice down,' she snapped. The eyes and ears of the three or four other people in their semiprivate hostel room turned in their direction. Earlier in the week, Tereza had attempted to create privacy by stretching their luggage vertically in front of their rented bunkbed, where she and Arsen slept on the bottom and Milo on top. This had only made them more curious to the assortment of backpackers and budget-minded travellers rotating in and out of the place night after night. 'Why don't you just use your earnings from the day to get something from that vending machine in front of the building? I mean, you *know* that your father and I need date nights occasionally. Private meals between the two of us.'

The muteness Milo had verged on only moments before erupted into shades of fuchsia laced with the smell of arsenic. 'He's not my fucking father!'

They did not lock eyes, but Milo felt the burst coming even before Arsen's soiled hand slapped the side of his face.

Arsen said nothing. He hadn't needed to. Milo snatched his rucksack and dashed out of the room.

Outside, the sky turned grey, and the mosquitos multiplied. Milo stared at the vending machine. His appetite had vanished, but he wouldn't go back in, not for a while, not until it was safe to climb into the top bunk unbothered. He sat on a concrete pillar separating the building's parking lot from the road in front.

The light from a single halogen streetlamp flickered overhead. A shadow appeared, followed by a voice.

'You all right?' The voice was husky, coloured by frat parties and pot.

Milo looked up. A man with dirty-blonde hair and eyes the shade of the Mediterranean smiled at him. The gentleness of his face did not match the creases in his voice. He seemed much older than the twenty-something he must have been.

'What's it to you?' He hadn't meant for the phrase to come out too harsh, but he was in no mood for chitchat.

The man took one step closer and held his toothy smile. 'Ugh, nothing?'

Milo realised now that this stranger had some kind of American Southern accent, the kind actors in old black-and-white films had. This was a happy memory: being seven or eight years old, watching Westerns with his father. His real father.

'I mean, I saw what happened in there, so I came out 'ere to check on ya.'

Milo twisted his face into something resembling a smile. It was the best he could do under the circumstances. 'Oh...well...that's cool of you.'

The man pointed to the cinderblock next to Milo. 'Mind if I sit down?'

The half-smile on Milo's face exploded in a full-blown grin. He couldn't remember his last real conversation.

'I'm Daniel.'

'Milo.'

'How long you been staying here?'

'Not long.'

'How old are you?'

'Seventeen.'

Daniel's gentle expression and toothy smile at once vanished. This young man, this boy, this Milo had looked much younger at first. Thirteen, maybe, fourteen. His face was smooth, his voice almost prepubescent, his whole bodily structure of bones and teeth and hair screamed underdeveloped.

'You want something to eat? I've got some leftovers in the kitchen on the first floor, assumin' one of those hungry Eastern European backpackers ain't helped 'emselves.' Daniel contorted his lips into a smile again.

'Don't need any handouts,' Milo sighed, unconvinced. He hadn't felt ill at ease taking food from strangers in a long time, but those were randoms, people he'd never likely see again and never had to speak with. But he didn't know or trust this man's intentions.

'Nah, didn't mean it that way... Look, I'm lonely too, so if you wanna eat with me... that's all.'

They sat for some moments staring at the headlights of passing cars.

At last, Milo gave in. 'Yeah, all right then.' He had to eat.

VIII.

Terence woke dripping with salty, red sweat. The Egyptian cotton sheets felt damp on his legs. His boxer shorts stuck to the insides of his thighs like cling film drawn tightly over a container. He stared at the clock on the nightstand. Christ, it was only 5:00 a.m., but he wouldn't be able to get back to sleep again after that nightmare. It felt too real. Realer than real. The boy, starving, emaciated, coming toward him with out-stretched arms. Arms of death holding a mangled top hat, eyes of fire. A coarse and sickened voice: *Change, can you spare some change? Hungry, I'm hungry.* And then dropping the top hat, Terence saw himself run-ning away, tripping over the hat, the boy not moving but always one step behind, the hoarseness of his voice echoing. Hungry, I'm hungry.

It had been enough to scare Terence, scare him in a way that he thought only children could be frightened by dreams. He would give the boy some change today.

He didn't believe in hauntings; he knew it wasn't really the homeless boy come to him in his sleep. But he'd do it, anyway. He'd go to the cashpoint, withdraw some paper, and split the change at Coffee, leaving more than a few coins for the boy with the top hat.

'You came back!' James looked out from behind the countertop.

'And with cash this time,' said Terence, smiling.

As the barista prepared a double mocha, Terence surveyed the small shop. He was the only patron. 'Business tough with the green lady up the street?' He motioned toward his old favourite chain.

'People don't seem to want to support small business much, but we get a good crowd around lunchtime, people too impatient to wait in line for the manufactured stuff.'

They exchanged a knowing smile as James handed Terence his coffee.

'What do you do? If you don't mind my asking. I saw you banging away at that laptop of yours yesterday.'

'That's right. I'm a writer.'

'Anything I might know?'

There it was. The question every writer dreads. Would you know, for example, the first novel I published, which sold less than a hundred copies? Or the second, which sold ten times as many but got shitty reviews? No, how about the third?

'*Noon at the Louvre.*'

'Oh! I read that. Good story; reminded me of what's happening in Whitehall at the moment. The corruption and bribery and—'

'Hey, what do you know about the homeless kid begging across the street?' Terence was not sorry to cut James off. Talking about his work was one thing. Talking about it in the context of politics was quite another.

'Oh, um, I don't know. Only been there a couple days, I think. Actually, he came in here yesterday afternoon, sometime after you'd left. Bought an energy bar. Or tried to. I felt so bad for a kid that age having to beg on the streets, I gave it to him for free.'

'You give a lot out for free, don't you?'

'Only what I can afford... The kid couldn't be over thirteen, I'd guess. Ought to be in school, not worrying about where his next meal's coming from... Why do you ask?'

'I tripped over his hat yesterday. The hat he uses to collect change. I guess I feel bad for it.'

'Well, I wouldn't. The homeless always do that, leave their paper cups or whatever in the middle of the pavement. I think it's a tactic, to get people to see them more easily.'

'Oh well, nevertheless...'

Three pounds fifty in change. That would be plenty to ease his guilt and to make a dent in the boy's collection. How much could he expect in a day, anyway? Five or ten pounds?

Terence left Coffee an hour later, and after walking directly across the street, he dropped a two-pound coin, a one-pound coin, and a fifty-pence piece into the top hat, letting his eyes wander up a few centimetres to have a brief look at the boy's face.

IX.

The almost-new novel had sat unopened on Milo's lap the whole way to New Bond Street. He couldn't get his mind to concentrate on the political machinations of people remote from his own circumstances. Not when he had more interesting preoccupations. He and Daniel had gone back to the bunkroom around 11:30 the night before, Milo crawling step-by-step, slowly and evenly up the ladder to his mattress, careful not to stir the adults below. Once he'd tucked himself beneath the grit of the yellowed sheets, he'd turned his head toward the bunk opposite. Daniel lay there smiling as toothy a smile as he had when they'd met outside by the vending machine. And what was more, he'd asked no more questions that night. They'd gone about making dinner—chopping lettuce, throwing raw vegetables over it, splashing olive oil on top—and still no questions. No 'Where are you from?' or 'What are you doing here?' Not through the salad and not even through the reheated spaghetti served in equal portions in two plastic bowls. Daniel spoke of himself but asked no questions.

'Imma travelling through Europe,' he said in his Southern drawl, 'on account of havin' just finished college.'

Milo's eyes went wide. He'd known no one his own age with a tertiary education. 'You mean "university"?'

Daniel nodded. 'Same thing.'

Milo supposed that anyone on an epic adventure like Daniel's would look for opportunities to make connections. There might be a tendency to embellish one's story and to forget to ask about the life of his listener. And partly, Milo was glad for this. He was reticent, even ashamed, to say anything of his past, and even less about his present. But another part of him wanted exactly that: to share everything, to at last unburden himself. And to a kind stranger? Even better.

Milo's heart jumped in his ribcage every time he thought of Daniel, which had to have been almost a hundred times already that morning.

New Bond Street was dead by the time Milo arrived to set up his station in the same spot as the day before. It wouldn't be long before the usual crowds filed by, and Milo sat hoping there would be more variety, some different faces than those who had donated yesterday and thus were unlikely to give again today.

Hours passed. Milo fixed his gaze on the balustrade of a building opposite, only breaking his stare to transfer money from the top hat to his pockets. But at mid-morning, a miracle occurred (not that he believed in miracles any more than he believed in the god he prayed to). A man, a familiar face, passed by, dropping a handful of large, heavy coins that clanged as they hit one another. The man paused for only a second or two, long enough that Milo's concentration broke as he moved his eyes from the stony balustrade to notice the cool trepidation of this generous benefactor.

X.

Heading home on the bus, Milo stared at the back cover of the almost-new paperback. Maybe there were miracles. That was him; it had to be him. 'Damn,' he said aloud, unnerving the middle-aged, white woman sitting in front of him. She looked back, noticed his peculiar clothes and the look about him—the look of a crazy person or a poor person, she didn't know or care which—and promptly moved to the other side of the bus. Milo didn't mind because what were the odds that the author of the book he'd fished at random from between the dirty seats of a double-decker would walk by him on New Bond Street of all places and notice him, leave money, and make eye contact. Too many coincidences for it not to be a miracle. And if there were miracles, did that mean there was a god?

Milo remembered that he had felt this way before. *Once upon a time*, he thought, because it felt so distant, like a fairy tale that had happened to someone else, someone more enchanted. But it was coming back to him now.

In those days, his mother still worked. A real, out-of-the-house job that had nothing to do with accounting for the daily beggar's budget. Before Arsenije or any of the others, Tereza had been a nurse. Milo had walked through the front door of their terraced Georgian row house at 3:30, the school bus having let him off just across the street.

'You're home early, son.' His father's soft voice called from the end of the hall, where his study was situated.

'How'd you know it was me, Daddy?' ten-year-old Milo called, throwing off his jumper and school-regulation boat shoes at the same time.

'Who else would it be?' It was this unlikely compound of sweet honey tones on top of deep amber vibrato that Milo remembered best. That kind of voice always feels caring even when it is angry or chastising.

'Mummy at work?'

'Afternoon and evening today. Double shift.'

'Can you help me with my homework?'

'Course I can.' A man as large as his voice was deep appeared in the hallway. As his father strode toward him, Milo smiled and stretched out his arms for a hug. Of his two parents, he liked his daddy best. Milo knew it wasn't right to say that out loud, but it was true.

He settled on: 'I'm glad you're here, Daddy.'

'Ah well, I've got a bit of writer's block today, and anyway I'm always happy to see you, son.'

School, homework, his father. He'd had almost a whole year of that: Tereza working the three-to-eleven shift. He didn't miss her because his father would help Milo with his homework. The next year, though, everything changed. Tereza still worked the same hours, but Milo now came home to any empty house.

At the end of the corridor, the empty study was another reminder that the tall man with the caring voice had disappeared.

It had taken Tereza a few days to notice. It wasn't unusual for her husband to fall asleep in his study or to come to bed late. She rarely paid attention. After work, she often met friends for a drink or caught late-night films at the cinema or hung out at the billiards hall downtown. Anything to cling to a little semblance of the single life she could no longer have. By the time she'd come home at 2:00, sometimes 3:00 a.m., her only concern was to take a shower, peek into Milo's room, and crawl into bed. Whether her husband happened to be there made no difference. By the third night, though, she'd sensed something was wrong. None of the girls were up for a drink, and she wasn't up for anything else, so at 11:30 when Tereza arrived home, she had expected to find him in his study or in the basement television room. She was in the mood for a shag and perhaps he was, too. This was, she considered, one of the only perks to being married.

Milo had woken to the back and forth shaking on his shoulder and his mother's voice.

'Where's your father, Milo?'

'Dunno, Mummy.'

'What'd he make you for your tea?'

'I got it for myself.'

'Why? What was he doing?'

'Dunno. He isn't here.'

'When did he leave?'

'I dunno, Mummy. Didn't see him since Monday. Or Sunday? He wasn't here on Monday when I got in from day camp.'

'You sent yourself off to camp?'

'Yeah. Daddy doesn't like to be disturbed in the mornings. Says he does his best writing then.'

'And you haven't seen him since Sunday?'

Milo nodded.

'Why didn't you tell me!'

'Can I please go back to sleep, Mummy?'

Milo scratched his head and looked up at the digital scrolling sign at the front of the bus. Four more stops, and then he could tell Daniel everything.

XI.

'And after him, after your father?'

Milo sat still for a moment, staring into the space beyond Daniel's head. Perhaps it had been a mistake to open up to him like this. Milo's mind had worked overtime on the bus, and at the first opportunity, he'd spilled it all out like nasty, green vomit. Daniel had kindly offered to share his dinner again. But now as they sat in the grimy cube of the hostel kitchen, Milo grew antsy. Now that he'd told Daniel about his father, he would have to tell him about the man after that and the one after him and so on, and then they would come to the core: why Milo was here and what he was doing. The very questions he had avoided yesterday. Puzzled and regretful of his behaviour, Milo shifted his gaze back to Daniel who was shooting another of his toothy, encouraging smiles.

'Well,' Milo began, 'first there was Seth, this muscular, blonde guy. I liked him least. Well, until Arsen came along.'

'Arsen is the man here with you and your mom?'

'Yeah... Seth was American, from some small Missouri town. And I never learned what had brought him to the U.K. Lured by work or something, I guess. He met my mother at a bar, I think. She went to a lot of bars in those weeks after my father left. One day, I came home, and Seth was there. No one ever said to me, "This man has moved in" or "This man will be your mother's boyfriend now." He was just there. To my ten-year-old mind, that meant he was some kind of stand-in for my real dad. And I hated him for that.'

'But you knew that no one could take your real father's place, didn't ya?' Though his accent betrayed him, Daniel's brow was furrowed, and he looked very sombre, as if he were saying something crucial.

'You think I'm dumb?'

'No, 'course not, but you seem like a kid who's interested in books enough to know better.'

'I don't know what you're getting at, man.'

Daniel sighed. He had only meant to encourage Milo. He was beginning to understand that this stranger had no one else to confide in. 'Well, you read a lot, don't ya?'

'I read,' Milo said plainly. 'Come to think of it, I got really interested in reading about the time Seth moved in. You know, looking back, it was a pretty peaceful time. Seth didn't pay any attention to me, and I didn't bother getting to know him. I hated the idea of him, and I loved books.'

'How long did that last?'

'Six months, maybe. He wasn't there for my eleventh birthday, that much I know, because I spent that day at the arcade with some friends from school. My mum said I could choose three. That was easy. I only had two friends, so I just asked one of them to bring a friend along. That was the last birthday party I had.'

'That's sad.'

Milo shrugged. 'I guess. Didn't really have time to think about it because within a year my mother was on her second boyfriend. This one, Frederick, was introduced to me on a Sunday morning. I was watching cartoons—must've been Scooby Doo, my favourite—and my mother came in with this old man. He had to be at least forty, and she said, "This is Frederick. He'll be staying awhile." Well, I don't know why she bothered. That dickhead Frederick moved out after a week.'

'Why? What happened?'

It started to feel like an interview, but Milo continued, telling himself he had wanted this: 'They had a big row, don't know what over, but I could hear all this commotion coming from her bedroom and then something like a loud whack and her screaming at him to get out and never come back. She was up in my room a few minutes later. Blood was falling from her nose, and she told me Freddy had gone.'

'Christ!'

'Yeah, well, what did I care about "Freddy"? I hadn't had time to call him by his stupid nickname.'

Daniel stood and walked to the other side of the kitchen, only four feet from the table and chairs. 'Gonna make a cup of tea if you wanna keep talkin'.

'Why do you care so much, man?'

'Hey, if you wanna go back in there–' Daniel motioned in the bunkroom's direction. '–go ahead. I just like the company and thought you might, too.'

Milo peered at the cheap linoleum tabletop, reminding himself not to ruin this, the only thing he had that resembled a friendship.

'So, after Freddy?'

'After Frederick...was Johnny.' Milo suddenly felt cold. Visible goose bumps ran up his arms. He would not let himself say too much about that man. He could not go there. Not past a certain point. Before Daniel had come into his life, before Arsenije and any of the rest of them–and before all of this, Milo's miserable existence on the streets–there had been only one person who Milo wanted never to think too hard or long about. Johnny.

XII.

The afternoon sky had grown dark, even darker than usual for a late autumn day, when the clocks had turned, and time had shortened. Milo wondered how he had managed to have a parent-teacher conference without either of his parents. He and Johnny were sitting on the concrete steps of Milo's primary school, and it looked like a storm was imminent. In fact, said Johnny, it reminded him of the how the sky gets just before a tornado: dark and calm. Eerily calm.

'How do you know about tornadoes?' Milo's voice creaked with the pangs of puberty.

'I know a lot of things.'

'Oh, like what?'

It was then, sitting there on the cool pavement with a storm approaching, that Johnny decided to cement his relationship with Milo. The kid was having a hard time; anyone could see that—what with his father up and disappeared and his mother on her second or third boyfriend since. And the whole change of life from child to teenager, a last phase of real innocence—well, Johnny felt something like responsibility toward Milo. That's how he posed it to himself: responsibility. He would show Milo how to be a man.

'What about girls, for example?'

Milo sat up a little straighter. 'What about them?'

'What they like, what they don't like, how to attract their attention.'

'Oh, I already know that.'

Johnny sat up taller. 'You do?'

'Sure. This girl Ashley is always following me around at recess and during lunch. She likes me big time.'

'I see. And what do you think about her?'

'She's nice, I guess. She tells me I'm cute, and she said I can call her my girlfriend if I want.'

'Is that what you want?'

'Dunno. She's nice and all, but most the time I just wanna hang around with the boys in my class, but they don't really pay attention to me.'

'What do you mean?'

'That they don't let me in, you know? Well, mostly. There's this one boy, Jason Cantone, who sometimes asks me to play, but I don't know the rules, so I look daft even trying.'

'Football? They asked you to play football?'

'Yeah, but I don't know the rules.' Milo paused, chewing over what to say next and how much to reveal to this stranger who only today seemed to take an interest in his girlfriend's son. And why today, weeks after Johnny had shown up? Why now, outside his school building under an afternoon sky that looked like it would burst at any moment? 'I don't really like sports, so it's whatever.'

'What sort of things do you like, son?'

'Don't call me that! Never call me "son".'

'Okay, okay, Milo... What sorts of things do you like?'

'Reading, cartoons. Mostly reading.'

'Well, there's nothing wrong with that.'

The sky opened up, and at last, rain fell like a living fabric. Milo and his new-found confidant moved under the building's thick awning.

'What time did your mum say she'd pick you up?'

Milo scratched his head. For what reason, he didn't know, only that he'd seen characters on the tele do that when they were thinking about something serious. But what had she said? She'd asked Johnny to go in her place to the parent-teacher conference, saying she had to work the 7.00 to 3.00 shift, and... 'I can't remember. Don't think she said.'

Johnny sighed and looked at his watch. He'd be late for the start of his own shift if Tereza didn't get there soon. He looked sympathetically at Milo. The kid deserved better than having his mother's boyfriend showing up for a parent-teacher conference. But Johnny already expected this sort of behaviour of Tereza, and after less than two weeks together, that was not a good sign.

'Tell me something else about this school, Milo. Your teachers all said you're getting good marks.'

'Well, Mrs Hirlea said–'

Milo spoke, but Johnny was no longer paying attention.

I don't know how I got here, to middle suburbia, Johnny thought. But it wasn't true. He knew how he'd gotten there; he just didn't know why. The how of it was that Tereza had been at the nightclub on a Saturday a fortnight ago. She stood out for several reasons: her skirt, which left little to the imagination; her top, which though skimpy, did nothing to give her the illusion of having the more fashionable, larger breasts of other women; her age, which in the scheme of things was not old, but was at least five or even ten years over the average of the other women on the dance floor. Most of all, though, she flirted. Without inhibition, without seeming to try, she flirted. First with his mates and then with Johnny directly, confessing after their first dance that she'd been angling toward him all night. And could they go back to his? she'd asked just after last call. 'Can't,' he'd said, 'live with my parents, in the basement flat.' 'You'll come to mine, then,' she'd proclaimed, but warned him to keep it down. 'Got a kid asleep in the room opposite.' Well, that was fine, but why had he kept it going past that one night? For this boy, was it?

'—and Mrs Hirlea told Jason that Tina said—'

A police car pulled up in front of the school building. At first it wasn't easy to make out. The blue, red, and black of the automobile melted together in the sheets of rain, but as the officer approached the awning, it became clear, like a Rorschach test that suddenly looks less abstract.

When they found her, the police officer said, she was sitting on a park bench with blood dripping from her wrists. The man spoke in soft, soothing tones, switching his glance back and forth between Johnny and Milo. After some time, Johnny pulled the police officer to one side and cut Milo off from the rest of the conversation. He'd heard plenty, though, to know his mother had tried to hurt herself. He visited the hospital two days later. It was the first time since his father had left that Milo had seen his mum without makeup, false eyelashes, or flashy clothes. With her work schedule and proclivity for living at the extremes of the sun's energy, he'd never imagined how different she would look unadorned. And, she had lost so much weight that he thought she might break if he touched her. He handed his mother her favourite brand of tea crackers wrapped in cellophane, which she tossed to one side of the tray next to the hospital bed.

XIII.

South Kensington always left Terence feeling put out. He wasn't overly familiar with this part of town, preferring the comfort of Northwest London or even the watery thoroughfares of the Docklands. Jean-

Pierre Mokrani's office was here, though, and on Terence's longish commute to the epicentre of French culture in Britain, he wondered what it was about South Ken that had captivated J.P.—apart from the croissants and baguettes and patisseries on every other corner. Terence hadn't seen his college roommate in over ten years, long before his rise to political semi-fame, so Terence couldn't claim with any certainty to even know Jean-Pierre now. Still, J.P. had never struck Terence as one for the stereotypical French froufrou. But when the bus stopped in front of a strip of French shops, it was immediately clear why they called this place Little Paris. *Epicerie, Le Marché, Confiserie de Connie.* The requisite Marks & Spencer was the block's only English saving grace.

'Believe it or not, this unit was standing empty for a while. That's what the estate agent told us.' Jean-Pierre wore cropped chinos and an Oxford shirt. Short, dark hairs poked out of the opening of the top three buttons of his shirt. Just looking at him made Terence a bit jealous. Here was a guy who'd had it a decade ago and still had it. 'The rent was too expensive, *c'est vrai.*'

'And, of course, you had no problem making the bill?'

Jean-Pierre smiled one of his trademark I've-got-this-all-handled smiles. 'With a little help from the embassy.'

'Well, the signage looks nice,' Terence said, his shaky hands pointing to the sleek metal plaque over the door. *Jean-Pierre Mokrani, Cultural Attaché.*

'Only the best euros can buy.' J.P. pushed open the door. 'Come through, *mon ami.* It's been a long time!'

Inside, Terence understood the office's high rental costs. Beyond the immaculate contemporary furnishings, the white marble floors and faux cement columns gave the impression you were in a renovated Grecian palace rather than a civil servant's office.

'Look, I wanted to thank you for all the memos. They–'

'Formalities, Terence.' Mokrani brushed his coat shoulders. 'Let's get a coffee, first, *non*?' He pressed a button on the wall, and in an instant, a slim male assistant who looked more like a twink porn actor than a secretary popped out to take orders.

'Well, they were really helpful in any event.'

'*Oui*, so I gather. This is your first bestselling book, *n'est-ce pas*?'

Terence nodded reluctantly as the twink reappeared with their coffees, wondering how the drinks had been prepared so quickly.

'And now you just focus on writing?'

'Yes. I left my teaching job last spring when I sold the rights to the book.'

'Ah, *très bien*. That's very good.'

Terence looked around. The office was empty as far as he could see, but the twink had come from nowhere, so it was hard to tell how far the space extended behind the anteroom.

'You've been in London for six months now, haven't you? Did they give you a staff?'

'Just an assistant,' said Jean-Pierre. 'She's an awful Welsh girl who speaks about as much French as Donald Trump. And a "butler," the boy you saw earlier.'

'Butler?'

'Manservant. Would you prefer I call him that?'

'You always did have a taste for younger men. So, all this space, and only the three of you?'

'For appearances, you understand. I suppose I could have taken an office in the Consulate up the road and had three times as many staff. But what would they do all day? Go to gallery openings, encourage the reading of French literature, eat decadent lunches ...'

'Trade gossip, in other words.'

'*Oui, mon ami*, and I'm afraid that's why we have *un petit* problem.'

XIV.

I'll ask for his autograph, Milo thought on the morning bus ride. But how does a half-homeless teen-ager/semi-fake beggar ask a famous author to sign a book?

Once, a forever ago, he had been a brave kid, hadn't he? At least, not such a desperate one. *Ask yourself why you want his autograph anyway*, Milo told himself, trying to talk his inner child out of the less than half-baked idea. To feel normal, for one thing. Normal people would want an author's autograph. And to show Daniel. To have something by which to impress this person, to show off and say, 'I've been places too. I've met people. Cool, interesting, even famous people.'

The last time he had tried to show off, Arsenije shouted at him. Arsen had been around five or six months at that point, and Milo assumed his departure, as with the others, was imminent. Milo had come bounding into the living room, where Arsen sat engrossed in the television.

'A hair, here on my chin!' Milo had said.

Arsen leaned in far more closely than was strictly necessary to examine the solitary but prominent whisker. He flicked off the TV.

'You think one hair makes you a man now?'

'Umm... no? But it's neat, isn't it?'

Reaching in closer still, Arsen put up one hand and, with the tips of his thumb and index finger, yanked the lonely hair from the pore.

Milo stood there, stunned and stone-faced.

'Well, don't it hurt, little man?'

Milo nodded, unsure what reaction his words might provoke.

'So, why don't you cry?'

And then, Milo did. Standing there looking around the room to wherever the first tangible, bodily evidence of his impending manhood had fallen, he cried.

'Not such a man now, are you, son? Not a man at all.'

On New Bond Street, Milo waited. And waited. Today, he no longer cared about exceeding Tereza's arbitrary daily budget or catering to Arsen's apparel whims or even about transferring money from the top hat to his pockets. Only two things mattered: something to be proud of and Daniel. And strangely, these two ideas felt like the same thing.

In the back of Daniel's mind was the thought that if he could do something nice for Milo, that would be enough. He didn't have much money. Every expense, down to a daily allowance for food, public transportation, and accommodation, he carefully plotted in the 'Notes' app on his mobile phone. There was no contingency. He had a return flight to the U.S. in three weeks, a trip to Paris before that, and then two more stops in France on his itinerary. There was no moving the trains and planes forward or getting out of prepaid hostels and B&Bs. Still, he could cut into the beer fund or perhaps skip breakfasts for a week. And an old friend from college had said that Daniel could call on his uncle who lived in London for a meal or two out. Maybe these rearrangements and little sacrifices would add up to something big for Milo. Nobody could make it alone. Daniel couldn't figure out where Milo disappeared to during the day, and it scared him to know the answer. He felt compelled to help in some way before he had to go. A boy could be lost forever otherwise, to a system where no one would show him something better than the four walls of a shared hostel room.

When Milo arrived that evening, all sweaty and covered with the grime of a London commute, a one-day rescue mission moved closer to the front of Daniel's mind. 'Hey, man. What are you doing tomorrow?'

No one had ever asked Milo this question. Of the range of answers from 'not much' to 'no real plans,' the truth was the only response he could not give.

'Umm… tomorrow?'

'Yeah. I was thinking we could go to the funfair in Central London. I read about it on my phone and–'

'Sorry. Can't.'

'Huh. Why not?' This had not been the reaction of a kid in distress that Daniel pictured in his rescue fantasy.

'Money. I don't have the money to go.' *A bit of truth couldn't hurt*, Milo thought, since Daniel already knew he was poor.

'Oh, you don't have to worry 'bout that. Imma pay-in.'

'Still can't.'

'What? I don't understand. Level wit' me, man.'

Faced with the choice to tell the truth to the one person who had taken an interest in him since Johnny, Milo froze. Everyone *wants* to be honest, but being forced to honesty feels like a dirty trick.

'I don't want to talk about it.'

The spectres of a half-dozen men swam in Milo's head, the plasma of nearly a decade of could-be and should-have-been fathers. Johnny, and his father's study, and the touch. *No!* he'd screamed at Johnny to stop.

Daniel could see the wheels turning, ploughing through the muddy waters of Milo's young psyche.

'It's got something to do with that Arsen guy, ain't it?

'Yes, in a manner of speaking.'

Milo's thoughts fled to the bunkroom, and some, even further away. And as his body froze, his memory took off.

With just one exception, all the structures on their block had been built as back-to-back brick terraced houses, all single-family, all with well-tended gardens and paved driveways. The exception was the house at the end of the road: a semi-detached two-story, stone maisonette that had the uncanny quality of being at once posh and understated. The tangible proof of her husband's success as a writer, Tereza had taken great pride, at least superficially, in the property. That was, until her husband left her. And while many of her friends, who had no shame in telling her, would've been content to own a house worth several hundred thousand pounds, Tereza didn't see it that way. She had never been interested in the actuality of things but only in their appearance. So, what good was the nicest home on the street without the pretext of the happy family to inhabit it? Still, she hired handymen, turned up for the occasional community board meeting, and kept to her routine at work, never missing even a day after her husband left, nor mourning the departure of her string of lovers post-marriage. Her peculiar responses to ordinary talk, to well-meaning friends and neighbours who'd invite her and Milo for tea or suggest play dates, slowly made her a stranger to the very people she had so hoped to impress. And yet, some part of her maintained pretences, for a while.

She was in-between lovers, and Tereza, just shy of forty, was thinking of a grand milestone celebration. To Milo's delight, she had traded in the after-work bar crawls and happy hours for more time at home. Milo returned from school one afternoon to find her at the kitchen table with a stack of newspapers and magazines, a large sheet of white poster board, and a magic marker.

'Come help me with this,' she said, and the two of them spent that evening rummaging through Elle Décor and Tatler and, oddly, The Daily Mail, looking for inspiration for what she termed a 'mood board.' Look for anything festive, she said, and Milo flipped glossy pages, stopping here or there to cut out pictures of party dresses and fancy cakes. This continued for two more nights until Milo's homework piled up, and he politely excused himself from this puzzling party-planning task. Still, he was content to have her home, and he brought his texts and workbooks to the kitchen table opposite her craft project so that the two of them could share a workspace. It felt good. Instead of using his father's old study, as he'd been inclined to do both as a refuge and as a souvenir of the quickly fading past, Milo embraced his mother's presence. His enthusiasm for the change, though, was soon replaced by an aching awareness that he might never go back to the study. After a week with Tereza spending all her before- and after-work hours cutting and pasting images onto the crowded poster board, it looked like she'd never move. Her fortieth birthday would come and go, and she'd still be there, gluing picture on picture in a never-ending collage.

Another day passed, and then Tereza looked up from her pile of clippings and announced, 'I'll have the party here.'

There was no point contesting it. Milo knew that look, the look of a parent who had made up their mind.

With so many things to do, Tereza flipped over the poster board and began making a list. For the next few evenings, a steady stream of workers and cleaners flowed in and out of their grand maisonette. It was a pleasant change of energy from the normally lifeless house. But the gardener, hired because the front hedges contained more weeds than butterflies, proved the breaking point.

He arrived on a Saturday morning with a beer in his hand and patches of hair on his face, as though he either wanted to grow a beard but couldn't or was just too lazy to take a razor to the clumps of dark blond foliage. Milo answered the door. The gardener—although he carried no gardening tools—grunted and asked if 'the woman who booked me' was in. When Tereza stumbled half-asleep to the front door some minutes later, Milo saw her face light up in a way it had never done before. Since her hospitalisation, everything about her had been, in one word, grey. Now, even wearing wrinkled flannel pyjamas, no makeup, and tangled hair, she glistened, fresh as morning dew. The gardener's rough exterior changed at once. He crushed the beer can and stuck the flattened aluminium in his jeans pocket, then moved one hand in a sweeping motion across his face as though magic might make him more presentable. Meanwhile, Milo stood there, slowly fading into the background.

'I'm Arsenije,' he said, sticking out the hand that had just crushed the beer can. His accent was foreign, though not welcoming in the exotic way strange accents sometimes are.

'Tereza,' she said, 'and the party is next weekend, so you'd better get started. I'll help.'

What kind of help would a paid worker need? Even thirteen-year-old Milo wondered. But the answer was plain enough: he needed ice water every half an hour, someone to hand him the tools he kept in his truck, and someone to listen to his incoherent stories in broken English. All tasks the eager Tereza took on. And then, repetitive days, simple and forgetful: Arsenije the gardener came back on Sunday and on Monday and on Tuesday, and Milo couldn't understand why his mother no longer seemed to work, nor why the lawn needed so much attention.

XVI.

The phone buzzed. It was Terence's driver, who was waiting for him out front. Terence picked up his belongings and stood in the middle of the anteroom, trying on his most pleasant face. Jean-Pierre Mokrani smiled back, unvexed.

On the long drive home, made longer both by the traffic and by the swirl of thoughts in his head, Terence watched the lights in buildings flicker to life as evening ascended. Across the Thames, shimmery blackness gave way to the glow of skyscrapers. And finally, back in his flat, he opened a box of dry pasta and put on the kettle. In twelve minutes, he had a basic but satisfying meal, flavoured with olive oil, flour, and salt. Basic was all he wanted now.

From the other side of the living room, a row of bookcases stood proud and foreboding. Terence had included his own three books amongst those by authors with far more popularity and success. The spine of his latest work, a black rectangle with a bold white font, stuck out with a kind of disappointed authority, mocking its creator.

The only thing to do is to meet them, Jean-Pierre had said, and try to smooth things over.

Terence picked up the television remote and switched on the international news channel, thinking the TV, which sat on the wall opposite the books, would grant some temporary reprieve from worrying about the future. It did not. Instead, he heard: 'We cross now to Whitehall where the British prime minister is set to address recent legislation designed to reduce carbon emissions.'

The screen split in two. On one side, a small podium sat on the pavement outside No. 10 Downing Street. The prime minister, a woman with flowing, red hair and without the makeup needed for television, approached the podium. Her face awash with the bright lights of cameras and news crews appeared sickly, pale. On the other side of the screen, a panel of three political commentators sat around an oval table in the news studio, interjecting throughout the PM's speech.

After about two minutes, a middle-aged white male commentator said, 'You would think that the prime minister would be more concerned with the accusations surrounding her marital infidelities than with climate change.'

'But she's been PM less than a year,' another chimed in.

'Well exactly, and already these accusations.'

'But they've been fuelled,' said the third commentator, the only female on the panel, seemingly unaware of her pun, 'by the wildly popular book *Noon at the Louvre.*'

'Indeed, one wonders what the author, this Terence Matthews, makes of the whole thing.'

Watching, Terence could feel the pounding of his heart in the sides of his forehead. He had known his novel was causing a stir. It had been the point to play on information his old school buddy fed him, to create a sensationalised political thriller. And it had worked: his first bestseller, the opportunity to live off the royalties. But it was all meant to be fiction, thinly veiled fiction, but fiction, nonetheless. And now Jean-Pierre was talking about a defamation case? Terence turned off the news and grabbed a cigarette.

XVII.

'Here, take this.' Daniel held out a £20 note folded into thirds.

Milo climbed into a seat at back of the train car and folded his arms. 'What, why? I can't take that from you. You're one of the good guys.'

'What's that mean?'

'That's how I get through the day. I think about the lot of them as bad guys. I know there are good people out there, but every time someone drops something into the hat, I imagine they've just atoned for something bad they've done, some sin. It helps me feel better about taking their money.'

'Kinda like you're selling indulgences.'

'Except in this case, the pope is Arsenije, and my mother is some kind of psycho virgin Mary.'

'Tell me,' Daniel said. 'Tell me how you ended up like this.'

Milo swallowed hard to prepare himself, to construct out of his jumbled thoughts some coherent story out of a messed-up situation.

'I watched from the front window as my mum climbed into Arsen's pickup truck. It was an early 80s model, I think, all rusted, with bulky taillights. "This is the best we have now," she told me, but even at that age, I was clever enough to know you must be able to have a lot more, or at least a lot better and newer, even with just a fraction of the money they'd taken from selling our whole "estate" at auction. That's what they called it: an "estate sell," but it was more like a noisy tornado that rolled through the house and took everything with it, leaving only Arsen's piss-poor truck in its wake.'

'Where's that truck now?'

'He sold it, later on. Needed the cash.'

'Go on.'

'Anyway, I was standing at the front window watching them get into the truck. Then, the horn blared three times. Mum was in the passenger seat with this look on her face like "Hurry up, boy," and Arsen was making some crude gestures.

'I got in the truck and asked them where we were going. You think they might've told me this before the auction, but I guess since they didn't have a good answer, they just thought I'd go along with whole thing, no questions asked. So, we backed out of the driveway and turned left down the street. I remember this because we passed No. 44 where the Jacksons lived. Mrs Jackson and her son, a kid that was in my year at school, were playing croquet in the front garden.'

Milo stopped and sighed. He took the tiniest pleasure in telling this part of the story because it was all about the life he'd had: a big house, surrounded by the kind of people that played posh sports like croquet, enough belongings to warrant an 'estate sell.' But he hated it too, because it was the end of that life and the beginning of the one that came after. Milo was seeing it now and feeling it again, through Daniel.

Mrs Jackson took great care and attention to decorate her home's exterior, and where she normally would have been proud to be seen, she turned her back as soon as she realised it was Tereza in the passenger's seat of the beat-up old truck. Tereza at once flashed her the international sign for 'fuck off.'

It had all kicked off when Tereza went to yoga on a weekday morning before her big birthday party. She'd only ever been to yoga once before, but now that she had the time and space, it seemed a perfect opportunity to follow up with the other ladies in the neighbourhood to ensure they'd received her email invitation to her party.

She showed up at the studio in her best Lycra, a second skin of leopard print, and white trainers. Tereza was many things: trusting to a fault, naïve, and even thoughtless. But she wasn't stupid. The lawyer who she'd found in the classifieds section of the local newspaper had promised an imminent windfall of alimony payments, which naturally meant she no longer had to work. So, she didn't care if the women turned to each other in hushed whispers when she entered the yoga studio. They were just jealous.

'Well, hello ladies,' she said, approaching them.

Mrs Jackson took a single step forward as the rest of the yoga mums stayed behind to emphasise her appointment as spokeswomen. 'Hi, Tereza. We—I—didn't expect to see you here.'

'And yet, here I am.' There was silence, a beat in which anything might have happened. 'Well, I'm no longer working, you see. My husband is providing ...'

'He left, didn't he?' Another woman had assumed authority and stepped to the forefront of the crowd. 'I heard he left.'

'Yes, bastard. Can you imagine? But the alimony ...'

'And what about Milo?' This was Mrs Jackson again. 'My boy says he's quiet, drawn into himself.'

'Oh well, I don't know.'

'You don't know?'

'Well, he's very self-sufficient, and I have a new boyfriend you see, so I, well ...' She could never quite seem to finish a full thought. The two-minute warning bell sounded, and more women filtered into the studio, laying out mats and blocks on the floor.

'Anyway, my fortieth birthday party is Saturday. You all must have seen the invitation.'

'Uh-huh, well, there's a church event that day, you know.'

'Oh, it's in the evening,' Tereza said, 'so you can just come over after that.'

'Well, most of us won't be able to make it.'

'Well, fuck 'em all,' Arsenije had said when Tereza came home in a rage. He had taken to sleeping over. ('Easier for him to get started in the early mornings,' she'd said.)

'I've had enough of this pretentious, too-good-for-us town,' she'd complained.

'Let me take you away, baby.'

And away they went. First to the next town, where they stayed for a few months. Milo took the long bus ride from the small flat they'd rented above the village's only café to his school thirty miles away, always making some excuse or another when one of the boys would (rarely) ask him to play football or to join one of the after-school clubs. Then, June rolled around, school let out, and Arsenije packed up their sparse belongings in the pickup truck, and they set off again.

'But why?' Milo asked. He'd not been a great fan of the situation, but at least it had provided some stability: the friendly faces of caring teachers, the sympathetic looks of his peers' mothers. And now they were going to who-knew-where.

'There's nothing here for us,' Tereza said.

But she'd never tried to have whatever it was, content to stay home with Arsen binge-watching streaming television shows, eating out practically every meal, and pissing off the nights at the village pub. Her biweekly calls to the strip mall lawyer turned into weekly ones and later into dailies, until finally he told her that her husband was nowhere to be found, and therefore, there would be no alimony.

'Well, fuck 'em both,' Arsen said. But with less than half the money remaining from the auction, he knew it was time to move on to other, more innovative measures in a town, any town, far from there.

Presently, the two-pound note was burning like a hot coal in Daniel's hand. He again pushed it in Milo's direction. 'So what's gonna happen if you don't give them money at the end of the day?' Of all the explanations for Milo living in a hostel and disappearing for

hours on end every day, the truth had been more surprising than Daniel could ever have imagined.

'Hadn't thought about. I was just planning to take it
from my secret stash.'

'Secret stash?'

'Yeah. I take the couple of quid I'm given back each
day and try to save as much as possible.'

Daniel put the £20 in Milo's hand and closed his
fist over it.

'Here, take it. Don't wanna hear anymore 'bout
it.' ('What you've told me goes nowhere,' he'd told
Milo the previous night, and he'd meant it.)

Milo's feelings for Daniel were growing. This
simple act fuelled the fire. Twenty pounds might as
well have been twenty million. He expected to feel
shame or apprehension. It was true, he had felt both
those things, but only momentarily. They had given
way to a catharsis that, when mixed with teenaged
angst, climaxed into something almost spiritual.

And then, here they were on the tube riding into
Central London going to the funfair.

TWO

I.

Terence Matthews, poised upright in his boxer briefs, sat motionless on the edge of the bed, save for the uncontrollable fluttering in his left eye, a nervous tic. He would have to get up soon and finish dressing, but he would permit himself a few more moments of silence. Just then, his mobile phone buzzed, the annoying alarm of a calendar reminder, meaning he had less than thirty minutes to get himself together. He felt certain he would be late; the car service was unreliable, and Downing Street was some distance away in rush hour traffic. Damn Jean-Pierre for getting him into this mess. If only the information Mokrani fed him had been more generic or diluted. He'd never asked for blow-by-blow accounts of the now-prime minister's tête-à-têtes nor had he cared for the specific descriptors of her liaisons. He had assumed those were clever additions made by J.P. to disguise their correspondence or to lighten the nature of their adolescent digital gossip. But this had been naïve, he realised, and moreover, it was lazy. Terence could easily have changed the context and characteristics: from J.P.'s 'Jasmine is rumoured to have met with the dark-haired, olive-skinned man outside the pyramid' to 'The blonde, green-eyed banker met her in the discreetness of a local café.' But no, he'd left it, changing only the occasional attribute, an egregiously thin veil.

Terence moved quickly to his small en suite bathroom, where he'd hung his suit on the heated towel rack, hoping to steam out any wrinkles. It was the best suit he owned, and he regretted not sending it for dry cleaning. It was the logical choice for that afternoon, but also, he felt, it was predictable and even would offer him some protection. He could forego the tie, perhaps, he told himself. A faltering, mournful sigh slipped his lips as he stared into the mirror, feeling sorry for himself.

He picked up his phone and opened the ride-hailing app. There was a surcharge, of course, and the agitation in his chest grew. He moved to the front entry hall of the building, flipping on the foyer light in his flat before closing the door behind him, hoping to provide something warm to come home to. For a brief moment, he let his mind anticipate what might happen if Jon and Jasmine Evans went through with the defamation suit. This flat, with its doorman and security system and in-ground pool, would disappear, right along with his ability to be taken seriously as a writer, never mind his ability to make a living.

The car arrived. Terence got in, mumbled hello, and put in his white ear pods, preferring the sound of his iTunes on shuffle to a potentially inane conversation with the driver. At least Jean-Pierre would be there to take some blame, perhaps, or to deflect the worst of it. Happily, there was no traffic, and the car dropped him on Whitehall five minutes before they expected him. Maybe some bit of fate was still on his side.

II.

Two miles and three postcodes from Downing Street, in an open space of parkland, Milo held a giant teddy bear in his arms. Daniel stood next to him, a plastic cup of Heineken in each of his hands. Milo had said he didn't want the rest of his beer. It was his first taste of alcohol and could be, as far as he cared, his last.

A few feet away, a mismatch of boys who appeared to be around Milo's age, perhaps students at one of the nearby sixth forms, clustered in a haphazard circle. A central figure, a girl one or two years older, wore a tartan skirt that looked like it might have fit her properly two or three school terms ago. She tossed her auburn locks, arousing huge smiles (and perhaps more) with every flip of her hair. Soon, a few more boys joined the pack. The girl became a satellite, and Milo could see she enjoyed the attention. A boy from the original group caught Milo's eye. Turning briskly to the girl, the boy whispered something into her still-tossing hair. She laughed subtlety as though appreciative but also nonplussed and whispered something back to him. Milo's heart froze. Who were these people, and why did he envy them so? The boy with his teenage muscle mass and scant facial hair, the girl with a smile big enough to match her magnetic personality. He suddenly wished he could take the beer from Daniel and throw it in their faces.

'Let's go,' he said, pulling Daniel in the opposite direction.

They'd gone on the tilt-a-whirl and drunk lemonade and been through the clown-faced house of mirrors and won the giant bear at darts. So much in so little time that it almost felt like redemption for the lost years, a childhood compacted into a day. It also felt like a reprieve, a break from a life contrived to benefit others, and also a glimpse of what could be. The only niggle had been those boys, especially *that* one, with his piercing eyes and secret messages. Milo looked up at Daniel, a whole head taller. That boy had nothing on this man. Everything Daniel did, he did with his body, his every movement structured and serene, if rugged. He even thought with this body, the miniature lines on his forehead burrowing deep when he concentrated.

As they walked along the inner corridor of the fairgrounds, kiosks and food trucks on either side, the sun began to set. A series of halogen lights that stretched across the roofs of the temporary structures flickered to life. By the time all the lamps had been lit, the dark circles around Milo's eyes had grown purple.

'What's wrong?' Daniel gripped Milo's hand, his southern drawl thicker with dusk.

'Getting late. It means we'll have to be going soon.'

'Your parents?' As soon as he'd said the words, Daniel realised his mistake. He could see the life drain out of Milo's body, his stature reduced in the haze of the hanging lamps. Daniel took Milo by the hand once again and gripped more forcefully this time.

Milo stood there, silent, refusing to look Daniel in the eyes and giving only an intransigent shake of his head. They stood in this frozen pose for what felt like an hour, neither acknowledging the other but neither letting go of the others' hand.

'Let's go over there,' Daniel said at last. He took one step forward, and another, until they were walking hand-in-hand to the rear of a food truck. There were no hanging lights here, only the faint and distant glow of the streetlamps lining the perimeter of the park.

'I'm sorry, man. I shouldn't be so sensitive.' Milo said. Despite feeling hurt, he'd fallen back on his inclination to be the first to apologise. This had saved him on more than one occasion from a harsh word and an even harsher backhand.

'No, no, no.' Daniel's voice sank deeper and softer with each syllable, the final one a bare whisper. 'I shouldn't have.'

'But you're right, anyhow, I've got to get back to… them.'

'Not before this.' Daniel reached around Milo, pulled him close, and drew his mouth onto his own.

III.

The main reception room, the cloakroom, and the prime minister's office occupied adjoining units on the ground floor of No. 10 Downing Street. As they traversed from one space to the next, first being 'greeted' (a kind way to label the security check) in the reception room and then depositing their belongings (including mobile phones) in the cloakroom, Jean-Pierre told Terence that it had been customary for most prime ministers to use the house next door to No. 10 as their residence, keeping Britain's version of The White House symbolic but not necessarily domestic. But Jasmine Evans had broken with this tradition, as she'd done with others, and now lived with her husband Jon on the floors above.

'And this,' he said as they entered the third room, 'this is her public office, where she greets guests and conducts meetings, but it's not the office where she works.'

Terence nodded in silly awe of someone with the means to share two offices in the same building. He wondered if the fact that he was being met merely in the ceremonial office and not in the real one was a good thing. In any event, there wasn't time to dwell on it. From behind the wood panelling on the north wall, a door opened where there hadn't appeared to be one. Out stepped the prime minister draped in a grey blazer, white Oxford shirt, slim-fit denim, and high heels. Terence sighed. His suit was too formal, even without the tie.

'Call me Jasmine,' she said in a docile cadence. She shook his hand as if nothing were wrong and asked them all to sit on the sofas lining a Persian rug in front of a solid oak desk.

They sat: Jean-Pierre and Jon across from one another, Terence at the other end. A slight glimmer of suspicion passed between Jean-Pierre and Jon, Terence noticed, as they waited for Jasmine to make the next move.

She stood for a minute, surveying the space, and then sat in a plush armchair at the foot of the rug, promptly kicking off her heels to reveal skin-toned nylons that just covered the rounds of her feet. Red toenails peeked through.

Eighteen years earlier, Terence had known a girl just like this who couldn't keep her shoes on. And even after all that time, he could visualise the shape of her feet: long and round, just like Jasmine's. He could remember their smell, too: artificial citrus like the fragrance of fresh mint soaked in hot water. He'd been nineteen and broke, hanging onto smells and shapes instead of nights out and material possessions. The girl, Meg, had been Jean-Pierre's idea.

That was the first good idea Jean-Pierre had had as Terence's roommate. For every hour Terence spent studying, Jean-Pierre spent at least two partying. It was a trend that Terence thought would be temporary, dying out from either a lack of funds or born out of the necessity to maintain high marks. But money never seemed to be a consideration for J.P., and although he never cracked open a book other than the glossy editions of FHM he left lying around their dorm room, his grades never suffered. For a while, the arrangement worked fine: Terence had the quiet of their room almost every evening.

But halfway through the first term, J.P. grew restless. He was still very much pro-party, anti-book, but his usual crew of mostly older guys from the Poli-Sci Department dwindled. They were busy lining up spring internships or volunteering at political party offices, and most of them, unlike J.P., were not from trust-fund families with cross-channel ties.

'Let's go out,' he said to Terence one night after they'd finished dinner in the school cafeteria.

'It's Thursday,' Terence replied, as though the chances would be higher of his going on a Friday or Saturday.

'*Ben oui!* Thursday is the new Friday, *mon ami*. It's happening!'

The bar was small and wretched. Urine-yellow stools stood side-by-side at a long countertop. Overhead, cone-shaped lamps cast circles of light in patterned patches. Terence had expected more, finding it hard to believe J.P. would prefer this dive over the relative comfort of their dorm room or the university's grand library. But as the place filled with collegiate voices and adrenaline-pumped bodies, the offence of the bar's décor receded into the background. It was the perfect setting for a short story, Terence thought. He sat on a barstool as J.P. mingled, working the crowd in a way that seemed at once French in its manner and British in its candour. Caught up in plotting how to weave this into his next creative writing assignment, Terence was only vaguely aware of the sound of galloping high heels approaching, until she was there, standing only a foot in front of him.

'I'm Meg,' she said, holding out her hand, 'a friend of J.P.'s.'

They were back in the dorm room within the hour, her high heels flung by the door.

The sole of Jasmine's feet hit the sides of her heels as she readjusted herself. 'To the matter at hand,' she was saying. 'I'm wondering if it was intentional.' She smiled coyly, serenely.

'If what was intentional?' her husband Jon asked.

'I was speaking to Mr Matthews.'

Terence saw the coolness evident in their interaction. Though he'd never been in a serious relationship, he imagined they all ended up like this sooner or later:

the dominant partner routinely and casually putting the other in his or her place.

The room shrank around Terence. Even the Persian rug shortened as he looked up at Jasmine. Her face carried that pleasant smile, but her eyes were balls of blue-green fire.

'Was it deliberate, Mr Matthews, your attempt to smear my image?'

'Well no, absolutely not.' Terence couldn't say, 'Jean-Pierre passed me notes like a schoolgirl—his observations and rumours from the political mill—and I transcribed them into fiction.' No, that would not do. He settled on, 'In fact, I wasn't even aware of the, uhh, similarities between my fiction and your real life.'

'You weren't?' She sounded genuinely surprised.

'No, you see I'm not that interested in politics, with all due respect.'

'But you wrote a *political* thriller.'

'Not interested in real-world politics, Prime Minister. I mean, Jasmine. I *am* interested in political plots in fiction.'

Some of the fire in her eyes began to extinguish. 'And would you go on television and say as much?'

Jean-Pierre once again looked to Jon, who this time kept his eyes fixed on Jasmine. 'I'm sure that can be arranged,' he said, turning to Terence and giving him a look that implied that he need only agree for the whole mess to go away.

'Yes, of course,' Terence said, though inside he remained unconvinced.

'Well, good. That's good, isn't it, honey?' Jon said.

'It will do, I think.' Jasmine reached down, picked up her heels and put them on. 'You know, Mr Matthews, when I found out you and J.P. were friends, I was sure we could come to an agreement. He's a good guy.'

If only you knew, Terence thought, standing to shake her hand goodbye. *If you only knew.*

IV.

They were silent for the first half of the tube ride south. The flush of a first kiss lingered on Milo's lips. It had been the best day of his pathetic seventeen-year existence, and yet he felt a strange melancholy sneaking up behind the jittery façade of first love. He was too mature to relish completely the fleeting moment; his experience told him that men are as quick to leave as they are to appear. The bittersweetness of it all, though, beat any day begging for change in New Bond Street.

The train descended deeper, bringing them to the other side of the Thames, closer to the reality of the hostel.

'If you're miserable,' Daniel said, not too delicately, 'why don't you leave?'

For Daniel, things were not simply black or white, but they weren't far from it. He was not prone to believing in infinite possibilities. He would allow perhaps three alternatives to any situation: the black, the white, and the fifty-fifty. Rock, paper, scissors for any decision. He made no allowances for something twenty-five or thirty-three percent grey. As he saw it, Milo could stay, or he could leave, or he could stop complaining about not leaving. That he *might* leave was out of the question.

'What kind of question is that?' Milo knew it was right of Daniel to frame it this way, but he had never thought of leaving *now* as a real choice.

'You said you have a little money put aside?'

'Only a bit.'

'You wouldn't need much. Leave, get a job, flip burgers if you have to. That would—anything would—have to be better.' Here was the third option, fully materialised.

Milo had thought of it before. It was a viewpoint that prioritised surviving over living well. It was a perspective held by those who had never had or wanted more. But he, Milo, had had more once, and he wanted it back. The corner house, the manicured lawn, the family, and the occasional school friend. Or if not that life, then something approximating it. People like Daniel, who'd probably grown up poor or slightly above the poverty line, knew nothing of this. They couldn't understand the luxury of the hoped-for, the once-had, the bitter taste of losing it all. For him, a trip to Europe with a backpack and a budget camera were enough and would always be enough. He'd be fifty or sixty and still showing his children and grandchildren photos of this trip, his one long summer in the old country. Unless, thought Milo, Daniel wasn't like that, unless he was different or honest or whatever word could describe the kind of person capable of tearing down walls. He had gotten Milo out of prison for one day. Could he break him away for good?

Milo looked Daniel square in the face. 'Who said I'm miserable?' (A test, he told himself.)

Daniel did not flinch. 'Well, that's obvious, mister tough guy.'

Milo was lonely; Daniel knew that. He could see it in every little action that dared to step out of the rigorous assembly line of the deceptive beggars' life that Milo had been forced to live. His loneliness had become his identity. Daniel wondered if Milo only stayed because he preferred the company of his mother and Arsenije, however twisted it was, to no company at all.

'Anyway, I could try to give you tips or something. I mean, I'm not from here, but if you wanted to leave, I could help.' Daniel had hoped that in saying this, he could begin to mend the awkwardness. Of the conversation, at least. They'd not talked about the kiss. And honestly, he had no idea what to say or think about that. A silent embarrassment descended on him as soon as their lips had parted. And the feeling hadn't left though they were nearing the final stop. It was a strange combination of shame and power: shame at their difference in age—small in the scheme of things but worlds apart in sensibleness—and power at the notion of playing saviour to this boy. Daniel felt his heart swell along with his dick and his biceps, so he couldn't tell the relative strength of one from the other. Fashioning himself a modern-day titan, able to cure all of Milo's problems, sexual, physical, and domestic, embarrassed him once again. He didn't possess the hubris to be a real titan.

'Anyway, think about what I said,' was all Daniel said.

They entered the hostel, climbed into the top bunks of their parallel beds and fell asleep. Milo would return to New Bond Street tomorrow, and Daniel would wait.

V.

He was staring out the window when the phone rang.

'Tom, it's J.P.'

No one had called him Tom (a nickname formed from his initials: Terrence O. Matthews) in so long that his first inclination was to tell the caller he had the wrong number. Now he recognised Jean-Pierre's telephone voice—the modulation of his normal, everyday, in-person voice that seemed put on specifically in case anyone was overhearing the conversation. It was a voice louder and more distinct because of the effort involved and sounding even more French for it. Another wave of memories from their university days rolled in. Terence gazed across the Thames at the high-rise buildings of Canary Wharf.

'Oh, J.P., *ça va*?'

'*Oui, ça va.* What have you been up to?'

'What've I been up to?! What do you really want?' Jean-Pierre had never made casual calls. In fact, Terence couldn't recall a single phone call in the last decade that hadn't been related to something J.P. wanted or offered. 'I'm busy, so get out with it.'

'Okay, chill, *mon ami*,' J.P. said. 'Why don't you let me come see you in a day or two? We can go over the plan for the interview.'

'There's a plan?'

'We'll make one.' Jean-Pierre sounded unsure, saying this almost like a question. But what choice did Terence have? Writers don't innately have the tools necessary for handling the media.

'All right. Tomorrow, midday.'

Terence left the comfort of the window and dropped the phone onto the cushion of the nearest chair. In the kitchen, he put on the kettle. He wanted to fill the silence of the flat, if only for a few minutes, by the steam and the whistle of boiling water. The stillness that he'd let envelope him since the meeting at No. 10 was disheartening. The first day had been fine: You-Tube and Netflix and PornHub had kept him occupied in varying stages. Day two, day three, day four each brought a successive and deepening depression coupled with boredom. The hours until the interview the following Monday stretched out and mocked him. The contemporary aesthetic of his flat was no help. Built in the last decade, it was sparse, hard, and too white, the kind of white that gets messy just after it's been polished but always bounces back to its original sheen. Offset by hardwood floors and granite countertops, it was the apartment successful thirty-somethings were supposed to have. And he had bought it with the advance in royalties from *Noon at the Louvre*. This only worsened its anxiety-inducing effect.

Terence had spent so much time in the flat these last few days that he sensed the white walls—decorated with art that could (one day, the gallerist said) prove a good investment—closing in on him. And although it had been a sensible idea to close himself in and take a break, so to speak, from life, by the fifth day he was reeling from boredom. Solitude is nothing novel to a writer. He spent the vast majority of his time alone in his own space and with his own thoughts, but he had always unconsciously relied on the small exchanges of everyday life to get by: a friendly hello to the doorman, an innocent eye lock on the tube, a brief but meaningful conversation with a shop attendant or with fellow coffee drinkers. Nostalgically, he longed for even these trivial pleasantries.

It was hard to know if J.P. realised the extent of the toll—psychological, physical, and otherwise—this was having on Terence, but he hadn't seemed to care much after they'd left Downing Street. 'You'll just go on TV and say that it's all a coincidence, and you don't care about the private lives of the prime minister and her husband, and then say you certainly aren't trying to benefit from this in any way.'

And, and, and, thought Terence. 'But that's not true, Jean-Pierre.'

J.P. winced. Terence hadn't used his government name in so long that it felt like a parent calling their child's full name when the child is in trouble. 'So, it's not untrue either. I said I'd give you some gossipy morsels that you could incorporate into a book, and that's what I did. They could have been stories about anyone.'

'But they weren't, man, they weren't. They were all about one person, one very important person who became prime minister, and you didn't even bother to change any of it or disguise their names when you sent me the tidbits.'

'*Et toi*? What did you do? Copy-paste!'

They had gone their separate ways, not angry at each other, but hurt. For Terence, a hurt that grew from his own arrogance and shame; but for Jean-Pierre, it was a hurt growing from a realisation that he'd gotten in over his head.

Well, thought Terence, once again staring out of his living room window, this time with a cup of tea in hand, *I will deal with him tomorrow.*

Milo sat on New Bond Street, willing *it* to go away. He'd been there more than two hours trying to place a finger on what 'it' was. He had woken this morning to see Daniel sleeping on the bed opposite, looking as if he hadn't a solitary worry. Part of Milo wanted to wake the man up, maybe even kiss him good morning. Tereza and Arsen were also sound asleep, so that wouldn't have been impossible to do. But Milo hadn't the courage to stir Daniel nor to admit to himself that maybe Daniel was right about finding a way to escape.

The commute that morning had only added to his funk, or perhaps, even set it off. Milo had started his ride at the bus stop outside the hostel every morning now for weeks. He'd never paid attention to the others waiting there. Sometimes he'd notice if there was a crowd or if there was no one waiting at all, which could be signs that the bus would be full or that it was running behind schedule. But he'd never looked at anyone, preferring to keep his head in a book until he was forced to people-watch all day from the discomfort of the pavement. Stepping on the double-decker that morning, though, it was odd to see only one other passenger. Usually the bus was so full that Milo was forced to share a seat with someone almost guaranteed to turn their nose up at him.

A woman had positioned herself on the upper deck at the very front of the bus, in the way that tourists and uninspired Londoners sometimes do to get the view. The woman's head, covered in grey flannel, did not move as Milo walked up the steps. He had half a mind to retreat downstairs but trudged to a seat midway down the aisle and opened his book. At the next stop, a man entered the bus, walked up to the top deck, and sat in the seat next to the flannel-covered woman. Milo couldn't help but notice this, and he began to watch them. *Did they know each other?* he wondered. But the two did not speak. Not a single word from South London all the way to Green Park where they alighted, walking off in separate directions.

And for some time, he imagined the two nameless, silent figures to be a kind of metaphor for his own quixotic relationship with Daniel. Milo knew that Daniel was adding something to his life—something he wanted to count on but was scared to embrace. Deep in the recesses of his imagination, he wanted to add the concept 'friend' or perhaps even 'lover.' But those recesses were not empty; they held an old, old sorrow. And who could tell how much more sorrow was on the way? Trembling, Milo allowed himself to remember, to go to those dark, filled places.

At first, there had been little things. Johnny would suggest that Milo wear certain items of clothing that 'you look hot in,' and once Johnny brought home a mesh tank top. 'Wear it when your mum isn't home, just for me.' At the start, Milo liked the attention. He felt special getting new things and feeling appreciated. But then, Johnny wanted to know where Milo was going and who he'd be with, things that a parent or guardian might normally ask, except Milo so rarely went anywhere that these questions seemed unnecessary, bordering on accusatory. Once, Johnny showed up to collect Milo from school. 'Who was that boy you were talking to?' he'd asked.

'My friend from biology lessons.'

'Lay off him, okay?'

A few days later, Johnny picked Milo up from school and said, 'I told you to ignore that boy. You don't listen.' His tone was so soft, so almost innocuous that Milo did not recognise it for the controlling, manipulative action it was.

At home that afternoon, though, Johnny stopped Milo in the hall. 'Stay downstairs for a minute,' he said. 'Wait in there.' He pointed to Milo's father's study in the back of the house. Johnny came back a few minutes later, naked, except for boxer shorts.

And now, sitting on the street, all the sounds eventually ceased to register on Milo's eardrums: the hums of cars carrying rich ladies visiting Tiffany and Cartier, the patter of businessmen's feet as they procured their midmorning coffees, the creaking sounds that dogs make as their owners walk him (a sound Milo believed could only be heard by street people who live on the level of animals), the thought of Johnny touching him. All of it grew still, like watching a silent movie. Perhaps it was the idea of Daniel that had made sound cease.

Milo stared up and down the road, thinking that although he had been doing this for so long, he had accomplished nothing. All these years, he'd assumed that he'd get out eventually and on his own terms. But for all the countless hours of sitting and staring and spacing out, he'd never thought to consider what would happen when he did escape. He had dreams of the lovely suburban home and the garden and a station wagon, but these were not dreams for a teenager or a young adult; they were the wishes of those robbed of a childhood. He understood this, as he passed his life in a kind of limbo of unexamined longings, knowing he would get out one day but not having a 'what then' in mind and not counting on anyone's help or guidance.

But who was Daniel to do it this way: to couple two things together, the kiss and his offer to help? Milo had equipped himself for the kiss. He had thought so much about Daniel, opened himself up in a way that seemed almost inevitable. He had imagined how Daniel's lips would feel, he had watched Daniel laugh and frown, and Milo knew every direction his tongue could move when he opened his mouth. But he hadn't imagined Daniel throwing him such a lifeline, moving up Milo's timeline by—well, he didn't know by how much. He only knew what kind of men waited in the world out there. Men like Johnny. Milo had always assumed he would *just know* when he was finally ready to break free, and he'd *just know* what to do, hoping Arsenije, like the others, would be gone by then.

VII.

Daniel woke up suspicious. *Loneliness is terror*, he thought. Whatever life is, it's not meant to be lived in isolation. And what could be more lonely than to lose control completely? He'd spent all night first contemplating, and then dreaming about, Milo's situation. He grappled with separating the complaints and whims of a teenaged boy from the facts of a desperate situation.

By the time Daniel had rolled over and opened his eyes, Milo was gone, but curiously, Tereza and Arsenije were still asleep in their bed. The hostel appeared a more surreal place to Daniel than ever, as far from his idea of a suitable family home as possible. Though he'd planned to visit the British Museum, he reached for his headphones, pulled them over his ears, and steeled himself. The Egyptian mummies and Byzantine textiles would have to wait another day.

'Don't be telling me I was robbin' *you* again.'

Through the haze of soft rock, Daniel heard Arsenije raising his voice to Tereza. He kept the headphones on but muted the music.

'Yeah, and how was your sleep, Arsen?'

'You ain't answer the question, bitch. Why your son isn't bringing in the money like he did before. Too little now.' *Toe-liddle-nah.*

Surely not, Daniel thought. Milo's guardians couldn't be using him to the extent Milo had suggested. Daniel had assumed there was a small amount of exaggeration to the stories, elements added by a teenager with an active imagination. Daniel tuned back into the conversation, cautiously. He feared being caught eavesdropping by someone with Arsen's bad temper.

'And don't be telling me I'm paranoid or some shit,' Arsen snapped. 'I just don't want to live here anymore. In a fucking hostel.'

'Yeah, it was your idea, mate. The bloody hostel.' Tereza picked up her purse—which Daniel noticed appeared to be in very good condition for someone of limited means—and walked to the door. 'Going out for a fag. You want anything?'

She came back fifteen minutes later. Arsen had taken out an iPad and was watching a movie. Tereza tossed a white plastic bag in his direction. 'Breakfast,' she said. They ate two blueberry muffins and watched the film in silence.

At 7:15 p.m., Milo returned to the hostel. Daniel had spent a good part of the day in his bunk observing the two characters who professed, in words if not in action, to being Milo's caretakers. As Milo entered their shared room and handed over the day's earnings, Daniel was eager to coax him into the common kitchen to share everything that had occurred that day: how Arsen ordered takeaway and ingested heaps of chicken and chips for lunch, washing it all down with not one beer, but two; how Tereza had been less greedy with food but went outside every half hour to smoke, announcing her intention loudly each time so there could be no doubt of her whereabouts; and how they seemed to have the best technology, the newest iPhones and an iPad that they used to watch movies without head-phones between smoking and feeding sessions. Did Milo know any of this? Daniel wanted to find out. Did Milo know where the money he collected was going? But Milo was climbing into his own bunk. He looked perversely laconic, and Daniel couldn't manage to send any kind of signal that might suggest they meet elsewhere.

Daniel had worked many jobs. He'd been a busboy at a Mexican restaurant during high school, a store clerk at a big-name pharmacy chain his freshman year of college, and a front desk receptionist at a boutique hotel near his dormitory in later years. But his most impactful job was at a summer camp for mentally chal-lenged teenagers. He spent three summers at the campgrounds in rural Maine, the last two as a counsel-lor. It was there that Daniel learned about the obstacles of communication with teenage boys. Many of the campers had answered in monosyllabic sentences whenever they felt challenged or threatened, growing bored with authority almost as a means of identity. While he didn't think Milo was mentally challenged in the traditional medical sense, Daniel speculated that his traumatic past had produced similar effects of shut-ting down.

'I wonder,' Daniel blurted to the air, 'if any of you know how to use the microwave in the kitchen? Can't get the damned thing to work half the time.'

Milo looked up from his bunk and across the room. 'Yeah, I know how,' he said reluctantly. He crawled down from the bed.

'Ah, good,' said Daniel, descending from his own bunk.

Milo faced his mother and Arsenije. 'Can I go show this man how to use the microwave?'

Barely looking up from their iPad screen, both of them flicked a wrist in simultaneous consent. Daniel had the thought that their lack of resistance had to do with the money they'd just received. Milo had served his purpose and was therefore free for the evening.

'I want to show you something,' Daniel said as they reached the kitchen. He pulled out an old Samsung phone, outdated by two or three generations, and opened the web browser. 'It's a painting by Munch,' he said, handing the device over.

Milo moved his index finger across the screen, caressing the glass. 'Is it a self-portrait?'

The intimate gesticulation of the finger startled Daniel. 'It is,' he said. 'How did you know?'

Milo shrugged. 'Looks like one.'

Taking the phone back, Daniel looked at the image more closely, picking up on its subtle contradictions.

The Munch in the painting could be anywhere at any time. The unidentifiable background gave itself over to the subject, who gazes at the viewer directly, his face and hands lit more clearly than any other element on the canvas.

'And he's holding a cigarette,' said Daniel, 'which was highly controversial back then.'

'Not exactly cool now, either,' said Milo.

'Did you know,' Daniel said, rising to the opportunity, 'that the two of them, your mother and the other one, smoke? Well, actually I dunno if he does, but she goes out a lot for cigarettes. I've been watching 'em.'

Milo pulled up a chair and sat down at the large table in the centre of the room. He put his hand out, and Daniel handed him the mobile phone again. 'I could have guessed,' he said. 'Is that why you showed me this?'

'No, I mean, what do you mean you "could have guessed"?'

'It's the way of the world, man. Some earn, others take and use.'

'It doesn't anger you?' Daniel watched Milo as though he were a character in a film, shocked at his complacency.

'I didn't say it didn't anger me, but—'

'You don't seem angry.'

The rules for what should and shouldn't anger people were not self-evident, as far as Milo could see. He might once have cared about such things, but nothing as twee or pointless as smoking could rile him now. And yet there were things that seemed to anger *them*, his mother and her boyfriend. It was a question of tone and feeling, Milo thought. He could be saying something totally benign such as, 'There weren't a lot of people on the streets today,' and this would be enough to set them off. Then, his mother's hand would come down hard upon the side of his head, with a blow that would send him stumbling back. But in other, more normal circumstances, she might have said, 'Oh, uh-huh,' as long as he'd given Arsenije the required £20. Anger was, in short, an unpredictable emotion.

'I'm done talking about this,' said Milo. 'So, how do you know about art?'

Daniel, who had been standing, took a seat opposite Milo at the table. 'It started when I was working at a summer camp. I was a counsellor, but the kids went to sleep early, and evenings were free. Most the other workers were people from the East Coast. Private-school educated douchebags and smart kids. I think I was the only one from the South, and my accent gave it away. Anyway, they all sat around talking about exhibitions they'd seen and artists they liked and the opera and all. I had nothing to contribute. There was no TV there, and the Wi-Fi service was pretty crappy for streaming, so I went to the camp library and took out some books about art. First, out of desperation to fit in, and then the more I got into it, out of real interest. That's how I learned about Munch.'

Milo lifted his hand off the table and began to stroke the image again. 'And what about the way he holds his hand? He's got the cigarette near his heart. That's kind of weird, innit?'

'Yeah. I mean, although he's looking straight at you, he also seems to indicate that he's looking into himself. And he bleeds into the background at the edges, becoming one with the nondescript environment and the smoke of the cigarette.'

Milo put the phone down. 'What do you think it means?'

'Well, let me put it this way: When I felt I'd studied enough to hold my own, I tried to get on good terms again with other guys at the camp. You know, start takin' part in their little night-time highbrow chats.'

'You carried one of the art books with you, didn't you?'

'Yes, and you know what they said when they saw me with it?'

'No.'

'They said, "You need to go to a gallery. You can't learn art from a book.".'

Milo laughed.

'You can laugh, man, but it hurt a little. I was trying.'

'Trying is enough. You should have just ignored those arseholes.'

'Oh, no, but you don't get it. They were right. Trying was not enough. How could I really appreciate the intricacy of this picture, you know, without seeing it full-sized?'

'But books are good, man; you could have learned a lot from books.'

'And I did, but it would never be the same as seeing it all up close and personal. That's one reason I'm doing this European trip.'

'What's that got to do with me?' Milo asked.

'Only that you've got to get up and out to see things for yourself, too. Stop letting fear or money or "trying" stop you.'

Milo didn't respond. He understood the metaphor better than he let on, and whatever had happened between him and Daniel at the funfair—the kiss and their connection—it all went into hiding at that moment. They sat staring at the table for a long time.

'It's hard, yeah,' Milo said, finally.

Daniel flapped his hand dismissively. 'I know that. What matters is that you think about it and act on what you decide.'

I'll never bring it up, thought Milo. *I'll never bring up the kiss.*

THREE

I.

Three important things happened to Terence on Friday morning. The first began with the ringing of his doorbell at noon. Or perhaps it had begun before that, weeks or even months before. But when Jean-Pierre came through the door of Terence's flat, a chain of actions ignited, the consequences of which were both immediate and life-altering. J.P.'s visit precipitated the second important thing to happen that day: Terence's decision not to make the television appearance. Their argument was so loud and so exasperating that Terence found it surprising, thinking about it later that day as he considered the third important thing, that none of the neighbours had rung up the police to report a domestic disturbance. And it had felt that way, like an irreconcilable tiff between lovers, building for days before erupting to a full boil.

'What do you want me to do?' Jean-Pierre had screamed, his voice becoming even higher-pitched than his Anglo-French accent. 'Call Jasmine and tell her you're backing out? She'll pursue the defamation charges for sure. We'll all be ruined.'

'Who is "we all"?'

'*You* and *me*,' he said with too much emphasis on 'me.' 'We will be finished if she does it.'

'You go, Jean-Pierre. How about you go on that programme.'

There was a terrifying glint in Jean-Pierre's eyes, as he realised he was being backed into a corner.

'Tell them it was all a mistake. You're speaking as my proxy, and it's all been a misunderstanding.'

'*Putain*! How can I go, Terence? How can I go? I represent France. I don't represent you, *mais non*!'

'Then I'll go, and I'll tell them the truth. How you gave me all the juicy details of the PM's private life in France before she was even an MP.'

'You wouldn't!'

'The hell I wouldn't.'

'*Je comprends pas*—'

'I would do it in a heartbeat, Jean-Pierre.'

'How can you do this? Does our friendship mean nothing to you?' It wasn't a real question since he knew the answer.

'You threw that away when you got me into this mess.'

Jean-Pierre stumbled backwards. Watching him was almost comical. He looked like a cowboy in an old spaghetti Western shot with a gun and taking a dramatic fall. The action, whether natural or melodramatic, calmed J.P.'s nerves, and his voice returned to its normal decibel. 'I'm not sure this will end well.'

'It's the only choice.'

Well, it's not, thought J.P. but it seemed they had settled the matter. He only wondered why it had come to this, or put another way, he could not work out why Terence had come to this conclusion now, two days before the scheduled appearance, when all week it had been a given that he'd go through with the interview.

After Jean-Pierre left, Terence let himself collapse onto the sofa. He'd had this piece of furniture for only a few weeks, and he'd decided at once to send it back. It was a reminder of what the successful book built on sordid tales had bought him. But he had also bought himself a way out of the interview mess. This hadn't been the plan. Terence realised its genius it was only when he heard the words slipping out of his mouth. The whole situation was J.P.'s fault, so let him clean it up. Still, a recessed, shameful part of Terence recoiled on the inside. He knew it wasn't *all* Jean-Pierre's fault. All the Frenchman's misdeeds would have been nothing more than gossip without a willing mouthpiece.

I've got to get out of my head, Terence thought and rose to put on a jacket. This newfound spontaneity emboldened him, and he knew just the spot for a little afternoon R&R.

II.

Jean-Pierre's driver was waiting for him outside Terence's building. J.P. got into the back of the car in such a state that the chauffeur, normally inclined to keep quiet, felt it necessary to ask if everything was all right.

'*Je sais pas*,' Jean-Pierre mumbled.

For someone accustomed to getting his way, the actuality of being bested, at least on the face of it, by a friend (hell, he'd even called Terence a confidant) annoyed J.P. as much as it angered and saddened him. The mixture of emotions, like the splay of paint on an abstract canvas, left him sick to his stomach.

'In fact,' he said, calling forward to the driver, 'take me to Downing Street.'

III.

Milo woke up at 6:00 as usual, turning over on the bed to face the wall opposite. He'd expected to see Daniel sleeping in his own bunk. They'd left things up in the air the night before, and Milo was unsure of how to set it straight. He didn't know if he was ready, as Daniel had hoped, to set out on his own and to make a clean break from his mother. But he also hadn't been able to come up with any good reasons to stay. Nothing he could vocalise at least.

He must've gone to the loo, Milo reckoned when Daniel wasn't there. *Perfect, I'll go find him and apologise and let him know how much his friendship means to me. And a kiss*, he added. *Maybe I'll sneak a second kiss.* But Daniel wasn't in the loo. Nor was he in the kitchen, or in the common lounge, or outside at the smoking patio. Milo would be late getting into Central London.

IV.

Jon Evans paced the Berber carpet of their lounge in No. 10. Downing Street. Jean-Pierre was on his way, which meant trouble but also meant something far more sinister: it reminded Jon that he was no better than this wife. Okay, maybe a bit better. He hadn't stepped out of the marriage with god-only-knows how many men (and a woman too, if the rumours were true). But what he had done was also a betrayal of trust. It had been all right, a justifiable offence, when he thought she wouldn't find out it was him who had leaked the information. He hadn't counted on Mokrani being so daft as to pass it all word-by-bloody-word to Terence O. Matthews. He'd only meant Jean-Pierre to give Matthews a flavour and then let him invent the rest, just enough salaciousness to alert Jasmine that someone was onto her but not enough that the source could be traced. Now, the only narrative Jon could use as a masquerade was to convince Mokrani to play dumb. Everyone had to keep acting as though they knew nothing, that it was all one big coincidence. Then, perhaps, Jasmine would give up and move on. After all, weren't there bigger problems in Westminster to solve?

But Stephanie, their baby girl Stephanie. Even five years later, the thought of her death felt like nails running up his arms. He had dealt with it in all the normal ways—as normal as one can deal with the loss of a six-month-old—by enrolling in grief counselling, attending support group meetings, and writing in a journal all the things he had hoped, one day, to say to her. But Jasmine had gone another route: trading psychiatry for sexology. Using their self-imposed sojourn to Paris not to recover or to forget, as she'd promised to do, but to gallivant. It was as though a whole new world of scarf-wearing, croissant-eating men had offered her a life-line, bringing colour to a world devoid of her dead baby and the husband whose neglect might have killed her. Jon's guilt ate at him, and though the doctors had assured him that any baby could die of SIDS, he couldn't shake the feeling that had he only watched her a little more closely or had he not put her down for a nap, Stephanie would be alive now, a thriving primary schooler.

Jean-Pierre looked browbeaten as he stepped through the door. Never before, in their months of liaisons since first meeting at Jasmine's big speech, had Jon ever seen him look anything other than utterly polished and presentable. Soon enough, the reason had become clear.

'Why is he refusing to do the show?'

'*Je sais pas*. He didn't give a reason.'

'Well, threaten him. Did you threaten him? The defamation suit—'

'He doesn't seem to care. In fact, he said he'd come out with all of it, how I gave him the information, etcetera.'

'He knows?'

'*Mais non*, not about *you*, but he knows enough to make me a political piranha. I don't think it would be hard for Jasmine to figure out where I got my information.'

Jon shook his head. 'That bitch.' The security operative guarding the room at this assigned location turned his head quickly and then turned it back again.

'Better keep it down, *mon ami*. Don't want another gossiper on your hands in that one.'

Yes, because you and I are not enough, are we? thought Jon.

'Well, what are we to do?'

'I'll go...'

As Jean-Pierre spoke of his plans, Jon couldn't help but feel an anger rising in him directed at this man. Five years after Stephanie's death, and no one talked about it. Most people didn't even know about it, and yet it had caused all this—Jasmine's affairs, and Jon's spying, and his petty revenge. Who gets revenge on their wife by asking someone to ask someone else to write a book about her secrets? And now Jon felt, for the first time, some sympathy for Jasmine. It was stu-

pid, he knew, to overlook her infidelities, and yet
mightn't he have found himself in the same place, making the same decisions if he hadn't dealt with the grief
as hastily or hadn't tried to suppress it? It had never
crossed his mind to show her any forgiveness beyond
the duty he'd promised in standing beside her, the Hil-
lary to her Bill. And yet his chance would never come,
he knew, in the way it had for that former first lady. Not
that he wanted a life of politics for himself. No, this life
was enough, serving as her backbone and speechwriter
and background policy advisor. It would be enough, if
only he could have all of her.

'Okay,' he'd turned to Mokrani, 'you go, and I'll
handle Jasmine.'

Oh, he'd handle her all right, and it would start by
telling her the truth. Fuck Mokrani and his machinations, and fuck his puppet Matthews, too.

V.

Falling apart. Milo was falling apart. He felt a great
distance opening up between him and Daniel. Daniel
had seen Milo's vulnerability but had not, unlike most
of the men Milo had known, tried to exploit it. Not yet.
Milo only hoped that his assumption was wrong, that

Daniel had not walked out on him. He realised this, sitting on his usual corner of New Bond Street. It had felt like manipulation, Daniel's attempts to convince Milo to leave, but it had not been that. It had been concern, maybe even caring. But how can you know this when every man you've known has tried to use you or leave you? Even his own father, and even Johnny. Suddenly, the thought of Johnny triggered something deep within Milo. He measured time by relationships. The last couple years meant the age of Arsenjie, a terrible period. The Johnny epoch he always chose to think of as a comparatively benign one, on the whole. When you think of time in this way, there isn't room for anything other than binaries: good and bad. But now, Milo sensed something beyond that duality. Yes, Johnny had been nice. But nice does not mean good.

And what of this present time dominated by Daniel? When their relationship, so unlikely begun, survived the first encounter, when Milo's shy, almost brutal affection revealed itself, and when it progressed to the kiss, his shame at his past, his feelings for boys never acknowledged, his whole plan for 'getting out' tossed in his face, Milo felt the winds of fear lurking behind his own bravado.

Meanwhile, Daniel had rediscovered the truth about boys that he'd forgotten in his four years of university: rationality—acting in one's own best self-interest—is not something you can expect a seventeen-year-old to comprehend. So, he'd gathered his things into his backpack and checked out of the hostel early. He would have leave at some point; better to do it before his feelings for Milo developed any further. Except, as teenage boys are wont to do, Milo had already fallen for Daniel.

Despite Milo's initial instinct to run away, something had struck him about Daniel's manner of caring for him: the way he listened and tried to look out for people. He perceived Daniel's offer to help as positive, even though he had been reticent at first. Milo wanted to shout at Daniel: *Yes, yes, I believe you! You don't want to take advantage of me like everyone else has done.* Yes, Milo had fallen hard, which really wasn't that difficult to understand considering the cycle of move-use-abuse that was his life.

Milo was looking out into the abyss of London, fixing his attention on a single gargoyle affixed to the façade of an office building, when someone dropped a smattering of coins into his top hat. The clink of change broke his concentration, and Milo moved quickly to transfer the coins to his rucksack. He opened the top and unzipped the inner pocket. At once, panic set in. He couldn't find the matchbox, his secret stash. His body contorted as he got to his knees and emptied the meagre contents of the bag onto the surrounding pavement. The blanket, the cardboard sign, the Matthews novel. Everything was there but the matchbox. The pressure of the whole day tangled inside him like a knot, and when he let out a scream, the knot loosened and tears fell.

VI.

Mayfair, with its almost empty streets, shorter, stately buildings, and its little gem in the Coffee shop were just the thing Terence needed to destress. He carried a copy of Baldwin's *Another Country*, a book he returned to repeatedly, never able to finish reading it, but happy now because it had nothing to do with politics.

'Who'd you say that was again?' he said to James, the barista. From the window, he noticed the homeless boy.

'Not sure, mate. Been seeing him there most days.'

'Yeah, I think I've given him some change before. Can't tell if it's the same guy, though.'

'Well, he's odd, that one. He packs up every day around five or six. Today, he didn't show up until about half-ten.'

'That's observant of you.'

'Look around you, mate. Not too many customers; plenty of time to just watch.'

'Where do you think he goes?'

'Couldn't say. A shelter maybe? I kind feel sorry for the kid. It's one thing for an adult to be homeless, quite another for a child.'

The boy *looked* fine, Terence thought. Except he didn't know how fine a homeless person could be in a city like London. He took out a five pound note. 'I'll settle up here,' he said.

The walk from Coffee to the street corner opposite may as well have been a five-kilometre run rather than a two hundred-metre stroll, such was the time that elapsed in Terence's mind. Enough time to make himself sick all over again with thoughts of Jean-Pierre and the prime minister; enough to see this person he was approaching as a means of redemption, however temporary, an opportunity to repay karma and plant some seeds of better luck next go around. If Jean-Pierre had gotten him into this mess, then it was up to Jean-Pierre to get him out. And if not, there was nothing Terence could do about it apart from trying to be a better person. But he knew it wasn't so clear-cut and that he was not being altogether honest. J.P. might very well have caused all this, yet Terence had benefited from it. As much as Jasmine 'deserved' for some variant of the truth about her past to come out, who was he to have a hand in enacting that retribution? Or, more to the point, who was he to profit from it? He shook his head as he approached the homeless boy. This was why Terence dreaded the idea of family: families weren't able to protect their own from circumstances. This boy had a mother and father once. Where were they now?

Standing closer, Terence saw that the boy was older, maybe seventeen or eighteen. He appeared to be in a daydream, his vision fixed on some distant point. He hardly seemed to register Terence approaching.

'Umm, hello?' Terence's plan, in as much as he had one, was to drop the odd assortment of coins leftover from the fiver into the boy's top hat and to keep walking without a word. A silent good Samaritan. But there was something—what was the word?—'off,' perhaps, or 'mysterious,' about this young man.

No sooner had he thought the words than the boy's spell broke, and suddenly they were eye-to-eye.

'Wait,' said Milo, which was an odd thing to say because Terence had shown no movement anyway. 'You're that author of the book.' He reached into the rucksack carefully hidden behind his posterior and pulled out his copy of *Noon at the Louvre*.

'I am,' Terence said and wrinkled his forehead.

The peculiar way he had said those two words left Milo, who had expected something closer to gratitude, at a loss for what to say next.

'Where did you get that?' Terence asked, pointing to the paperback. Apart from feeling the uncomfortableness of recognition, he also wondered how a homeless person came to possess his work.

'Just found it,' Milo said reluctantly. 'And I like it.'

'Oh, well, I'm glad.'

He felt emboldened. 'I love to read,' Milo said. Wondering if he had lost Daniel made Milo grasp at the next person to show him kindness.

What an odd thing to say, thought Terence. But now he realised that he assumed homeless people had to act like goddamned animals. He had been the real animal though, knocking over the boy's hat and ignoring it. But Terence could not do regret. Sympathy was so much easier. 'Do you want me to sign it for you?'

Milo nodded his head.

'Got a pen?' And then, as if to recognise the foolishness of his words, Terence added, 'No of course you don't.' But by now Milo had already pulled out a capless ballpoint from his rucksack.

'What's your name?'

As Terence scribbled in the front page of the book, Milo's senses returned, his amazement replaced by curiosity. 'I saw you here once before,' he said, 'and you left me something. I had thought it was you, but I wasn't sure.'

Terence closed the book and handed it back. 'How old are you?'

'Eighteen next month, sir.'

'Call me, Terence... And you've been homeless how long?'

It was the question Milo feared. *Speed and strategy*, he thought. With a single, empathic gesture, he brushed his hand to one side. 'Awhile.'

'Give me the book again.'

'Huh?'

'Let me see the book once more.' It had been something about the boy's indecisiveness, the pale shaking of his hand. Terence scribbled again and handed the book back. 'I wrote my number there. If you're ever in trouble and need something, use it.'

FOUR

I.

'What are you saying to me?' Jasmine didn't know what he was talking about. All his words required a filter to sieve the useful ones and dissect them one-by-one for their meaning.

Jon knew that he and Jasmine experienced problems communicating, or rather, he felt she had a problem he was forced to deal with. He had seen it play out repeatedly in their years together. For all her political brilliance, Jasmine was not a skilled communicator of original ideas, nor was she quite able to understand the ideas of others without claiming they were notions of her own. A decade or two prior, this might have been an impediment to her career ambitions, but with the prevalence of social media, these days most everyone cared more for what she (or her delegates) tweeted or read off teleprompters than for the things she said off the cuff. When it came to their relationship, though, this inability to listen fully caused dozens of misunderstandings, including the present one.

'Dear,' he said, always finding it more expedient to use flattery rather than exasperation, 'I'm trying to tell you it was all *my* doing.'

'You told Jean-Pierre Mokrani about me... about my—' She could hardly bring herself to say the word *affair*. That word somehow made it more real, a shared term for the mutual knowledge of what she'd done. 'Well in any case, it's over now.'

'Yes, I know that,' he said, though it was the first time she had expressed anything like remorse, much less an apology.

'And the circumstances,' she flinched to stop tears from forming, 'being what they were, and ...'

Jasmine stared out the antique windows onto the cordoned-off street below. Though they were in the middle of London, she could make out no noise from the road. She strained her ears, hoping for even the faintest sound, but it was as though she'd gone deaf. It took her back to that other day five years ago, the day when all sounds had ceased.

The baby was born on 31 December, a welcome gift for the coming new year. It had been a relatively easy pregnancy. The usual morning sickness, one or two strange food cravings, and mobility issues in the last trimester purely because of the weight Jasmine had gained. But nothing like the horror stories of other mothers: gestational diabetes, or preeclampsia, or high blood pressure. Jasmine had gone into labour exactly on time, taken precisely five hours to give birth, and had done it naturally, using only Lamaze and fierce concentration. Looking back, all of this should have come as a stark warning of impending doom. But no one thinks that way. We're all just grateful for the small gifts, taking each thing that comes to us with little thought for the long-term payoff.

After a brief, eight-week maternity leave, Jasmine returned to her work at party headquarters. The country was bracing for a general election, and her job entailed working closely with the party leader to shape policy proposals. Jon (whose freelance journalism career had been rocky in the best of times) became the primary caregiver, looking after little Stephanie by day and co-parenting with Jasmine at nights, or better to say on the rare nights when she came home before the baby's bedtime. Still, she'd been good about getting up in the middle of the night and had always expressed and refrigerated enough milk to last the day.

Winter passed, and they fell into a routine that worked for them both, especially because after her party lost the election, Jasmine could spend more evenings at home. As spring rolled into summer, in the barely visible way that it does in England, so too did Stephanie develop: always meeting the milestones laid out on the baby growth chart given to them by the paediatrician. By late May, the baby still needed propping up by a pillow but was sitting upright for longer periods of time and had mastered a new trick of rolling over onto her tummy. She'd even slept through the night several times each week, a relief to Jon and Jasmine, who'd been, like all new parents, sleep deprived. And when, in mid-June, she began chattering away in coos and in 'babas,' and 'gagas,' and 'mamas,' Jon felt confident his little angel would grow up to be the smartest, most successful child.

And then, on 29 June, Jon had woken early with a long to-do list on his mind. Tomorrow, a Saturday, they were to host a small 'half-birthday' party, a celebration with cakes, teas, and coffee, in honour of Stephanie's six months on this planet. More for the adults than for the baby, of course, and so he had to visit Waitrose and stop by the party suppliers and let the cleaning service in during the afternoon. By 8:00, Jasmine had already left for work, and with Stephanie sleeping through the night, it fell to Jon to wake the babe and get her fed before starting his chores. By 10:30, Jon had managed to not only feed Stephanie but also prepare eggs on toast for himself. Estimating that he had enough time later to accomplish the errands, he took Stephanie from her high chair and carried her to the living room, where she sat on his lap as he watched a half an hour of Sky News. Stephanie, though, had other ideas, growing fussy until he sat her in her rocker, hoping she might doze for a while. This would work out well–he could gently transfer her to the car seat whilst she slept, freeing his hands for the drive into town–but Stephanie couldn't seem to fall asleep completely, only lulling her eyes half-closed before pushing the rocker forward again. At 11:30, Jon took her upstairs for a warm bath. This always worked to ease her occasional crankiness. After towelling her dry, they sat in the rocking chair in the nursery until she fell asleep in his arms. He laid her on her back in the crib and then went downstairs to tidy up the kitchen, eager to lessen the workload for the cleaners. More than an hour passed, and he realised he had heard no noise from the nursery. This was no cause for alarm, with Stephanie sleeping so well recently, but normally with the rest of the house quiet, he could hear her rolling around or even making some kind of noise as she slept. He went upstairs to check on her. When he walked in, he found her face down in the middle of the crib. Playing her old parlour trick, he thought, excited that she was growing more self-sufficient.

'Come here, pumpkin,' he said, reaching out to her.

But when he touched her, she was like the stiff cotton fabric of a bookbinding, soft around the edges but hardened in the middle. A single electric charge jolted up his spine. When he turned her over, her face was amethyst and ruby.

The first few minutes felt the longest as he tried to resuscitate her. Then, too, did the days and weeks afterwards drag on as the police carried out an investigation and autopsy, and before the confirmation of SIDS. Meanwhile, Jasmine had gone numb. That was her only option, she felt. It was either go numb or deal with the huge reservoir of unresolved grief. And so, Paris was the solution, their chance to start over. Not forever, but until they could learn to cope again, as two people rather than three.

'But what Paris was not supposed to be was your license to do as you wished.' There was no point in saying this again, Jon knew, and yet with Jasmine's weak defence, it felt appropriate.

'Yes, I know,' she said, to his surprise, 'and I'm sorry. I told you before, and I'll say it again, I am sorry.' Jasmine had been looking for someone to blame, someone to say 'sorry' to her. The more they talked about Stephanie's death, rehashed it, rethought it, analysed it, and cried over it, the more paranoid and spiteful she became until the only thought that comforted her was blaming someone, anyone. And why not Jon? He had been there in the house. Couldn't he have done something? Even when she'd done the research and spoken to the coroner, who had assured here nothing could have been done to prevent it, and that babies who are able to roll over are not considered to be at risk, still it ate at her, infiltrating her brain. *Stephanie is dead. She is gone. I might as well be dead, too.* And then, what she had wanted in Paris was someone with no connection to Stephanie, not the dead child's father. A lover with no feelings attached.

'No. No, you never said it before.' Jon was weeping now. 'You never said *those* words. We said we'd forget it, and I tried to, for a little while, and then... I don't know... the apology, the words, they mean so much.'

'I suppose,' she said, chewing over every phrase, 'that I didn't know how to apologise. I mean, I thought you wanted me to make some grand gesture, and I've been trying all these years to come up with what I could possibly do and trying to work out why you stayed with me, so publicly...'

'Of course, I was hurt that you stepped out. That you thought that by cheating on me you could fill the hole Stephanie left. Do you know what your cheating did to me? It made her death a thousand times worse.'

I want you to forgive me, Jon Evans, Jasmine thought. *For all the things I did, and for all the things you did not.* She was confused by this sudden wave of pain. She had thought that unlike her husband, she'd put it all behind her, stifled the emotion, and that Jean-Pierre had been the impetus for her moving on. Now, it was as if the characters in a painting, absorbed in their own concerns, looked out of the canvas and spoke to her. She could see how the decisions she'd made impacted Jon's life as much as they had hers.

An aide knocked once and entered the room. Seeing Jon crying, the senior staffer apologised for disturbing them.

'No, it's fine. What is it, Carl?' Jasmine said.

'The president of the Ukraine is on the line, ma'am. He wants to speak to you over satellite link?'

'Very well.' She looked at Jon, wiping the tears from his eyes. 'Tell him to give me five minutes, please.'

After the aide left, Jasmine put her hand on Jon's shoulder. 'You told Mokrani about my affairs in Paris, and he told that writer Terence Mathews?' Her eyes raised as if to ask if she'd gotten it right.

'Yes, and I'm sorry. I shouldn't have, err, aired your —our—dirty laundry that way. I was just so angry, and I'd been holding on to that anger for so long that when the opportunity—'

'It doesn't matter now.'

'But the defamation suit and the TV show—'

'Cut ties with Mokrani. Have Carl issue a statement that neither the prime minister nor her husband or office have any comment and do not deal in political gossip.'

Jon nodded. 'And us?'

'We'll be fine, love. We made it through five years of secrets and guilt and anger. We can make it through anything.' She put on a placid smile and walked out of the room, calling out for Carl to patch her into Ukraine.

II.

The hostel's dented metal door was heavier than Milo remembered. He was thinking of all the things he'd say to Tereza and Arsenije and, at the same time, hoping Daniel had returned. Though he knew this last thing was fairly unlikely, it gave him some confidence wishing for Daniel to see him stand up to his so-called guardians. But the room was empty. Milo realised this was how it might be every day until after dinner, the whole godforsaken place left to them as the others checked out or moved on. He climbed into his bunk and sat there, waiting and thinking.

Ten minutes later, they entered. Arsen was clean-shaven, smelling of soap and chain store perfume, and laughing as though Tereza had just told the funniest joke imaginable. It took them a moment to see Milo sitting in his bunk.

Arsen's smile turned to an instant scowl. 'The fuck are you doing here?' It was 4:00 p.m., far too early for Milo to have called it a day.

'Have I come at a bad time?' Milo said, mocking Arsen's gruff tone and eyeing the crystal-clear cufflinks on his white button-up shirt. Milo noticed that his mother was carrying two green and gold shopping bags. He'd never known Arsen to wear anything other than tatty T-shirts. And though his mother had, even now, maintained some semblance of cleanliness, Arsen was never too keen on a shower.

'Get your arse down here,' Tereza said.

'And don't mouth off to me,' Arsen added, although it came out like *may-of-toe-me.*

Milo didn't move.

'Where's my money?' Milo said, though it was already clear from the Harrods bags where some or all of it had gone.

'You been stealing from us,' Arsen said, growing more agitated. 'Skimming extra off the top.'

'Taking more than the fair share we give you,' added Tereza.

'I haven't.' Milo's anger grew, and he dug his fingers into the hard foam of the mattress to steady himself.

'And you thought we wouldn't find out.' Tereza stated.

'That was my money. I've been saving.'

At once, Tereza dropped the shopping bags and lunged at her son, pulling him feet-first from the top bunk down the five or so feet to the ground below. Milo was so taken aback that he stumbled onto the pile of blankets on their bed beneath. He might have predicted such a show of strength from Arsenije, but never from his mother. Before he could steady himself and stand up again, the full force of Arsen's fists reached Milo's face, and a quick kick to his chins sent him yelping with pain.

Just then, the front desk attendant, aroused by the noise, entered the room.

'Holy fuck,' the attendant shouted. 'I'm calling the police,' he said, backing out of the room.

The momentary break in the action gave Milo time to stand. A pain he didn't know was possible shot through him, but the rush of adrenaline fuelled his legs. He reached up to grab his rucksack. As he ran, he heard the clank of the door slam shut behind him.

'Hey, kid, where are you going?' the receptionist screeched.

When he opened the front door of the building near the vending machines, it took his eyes a moment to adjust to the growing darkness of a splitting headache. The air was aromatic with acidic overtones, like the smell of rotting garbage. All at once, Milo let out a sharp guttural scream. *Got to keep moving*, he told himself, scared Arsen would follow. Up the road, there was a service station he'd seen on the bus ride. His shins throbbed with pain, but Milo set his feet to running again. As he arrived at the service station, sirens blared as the police zoomed past.

FIVE

I.

Everything Jon told her, Jasmine was prone to believe. She interpreted his urgency not as fierce resolve to prove himself committed (which he was) but as ignorance. It was true she had broken off the affair in Paris years ago. There had only been the one, despite the rumours, but she'd be damned if Jon would ever learn his name. So, she'd made the choice to look disturbed or act shocked when bits of her past life materialised in Terence Matthews's novel. She knew all along who could have fuelled those allegations: her own husband, who, with his disagreeable voice and exhausting grief saw the opportunity to embarrass her, to get back publicly, and had found a willing ear in Jean-Pierre Mokrani and a mouthpiece in Matthews.

But now, for the first time, she held the trump card.

Naturally she loved Jon, even now. And she had loved their daughter. Jasmine had been tireless and imperious in not blaming herself for Stephanie's death. The man, the affair, had enabled that. If only Jon had seen the connection. She had had no desire to devote herself to a lover for anything more than a reprieve. His sex was the balm she'd needed, dislodging whatever anger she might have otherwise harboured toward Jon.

But it had made no difference to Jon that she took no pleasure in the relationship, no fulfilment of long-term value. He would rather have her torment and blame him than to impugn his manhood. In the end, her actions had quietly accused him. First, the *gardienne* at their Parisian flat had told Jon that a man had passed by looking for Jasmine. He'd not left his name, and the *gardienne* could say nothing about how he looked save that he 'appeared French, *monsieur.*' And then, Jon had noticed Jasmine, quite on a whim, outside the Louvre as he passed the Rue de Rivoli on his way to WH Smith. His first instinct was to rush over to greet her–'What a coincidence, and wasn't she to be playing bridge with the ex-pat ladies' group today?'– but then he saw the man's profile. Dark hair, tailored suit. Jon saw him lean in to kiss Jasmine, and he saw her eyes dart up to catch his.

Later that day, he'd demanded to know who she'd been with at the museum.

'You didn't get a look at his face?' she'd asked.

'What's his name?' Jon responded in such a way that she understood he did not know her lover's identity.

'What does it matter?' she said.

And now, in Downing Street, she scampered around her office thinking about it. How ignorant Jon was to use the very person responsible for her affair as his confidant. How very ignorant of him; how lucky for her. As long as Jean-Pierre played along.

II.

A long-held secret haunted Jean-Pierre Mokrani. He sat in his gilded South Kensington office mulling over his actions, trying to assign some logic to them. There was, of course, a matter of discretion. When Jon Evans cornered him at Jasmine's speech, he had seen it for what it was: an opportunity. Who knew Jon had been harbouring this resentment against his wife for so long? How dumb he was to ask his wife's former lover to help him exact revenge. How dumb but how convenient. Jean-Pierre had said he would help, discreetly.

All Jon had to do was tell him what he knew, and then he'd relay it piecemeal to a writer friend ('desperate for a bestseller'). But Jon's information was so far off the mark and so oblivious that J.P. had not modified it. Which is why, when Jasmine threatened the defamation suit, Jean-Pierre was more surprised at her coyness than her actions. He had underestimated her political hunger, her thirst for power and for being above the fray. Jon had rightly thought that Jasmine wouldn't want people knowing, even now, that she'd had a three-month tryst with a certain French diplomat known more for his penchant for pretty young boys than for his lust of older women. And Jean-Pierre too shared the need to keep it quiet, fearing it would ruin his social standing in the gay community on which he relied for support. But what neither had thought was that Jasmine would care if lies and half-truths were spread in print. Yes, they had underestimated her ego.

'Are you ill?' Jean-Pierre's assistant, the twink, entered the office where J.P. was mulling over his options.

'No, I'm fine,' Jean-Pierre said, though his face was burning red with perspiration. 'Bring me a Scotch.'

For a large part of the afternoon, he sat in the same chair drinking whiskey after whiskey until miserable and sick, he fell asleep.

'So,' he said at the team's working dinner that evening, 'I need you to get me an appointment with Jasmine Evans. Tell her people it's government business.'

'Yes sir,' the assistant said.

The smell of cheese omelette made J.P.'s stomach turn.

'Who do I have to blow around here to get a glass of wine?' An ironic question considering he'd been with at least half the staff.

Then, through his haze of alcohol, Jean-Pierre's disconnected thoughts took shape. *I have to get her to tell the truth*, he thought. The machinations of a drunk man are best forgotten. *Not about me, but about the liar I made Tom. No, scratch that, the liar he made himself. She has to come out with a statement:* 'An "internal source" leaked personal information to Matthews, which he then twisted and turned into fiction at the prime minister and her family's expense.' Discredit Terence. It was the only way to save them all.

Part Two

Homo sum, humani nihil a me alienum puto.
'I am human; nothing human is alien to me.'

Terence, Roman playwright

SIX

I.

It was the wide avenue that first struck him. They called it a *straße* here, and that seemed appropriate in somehow describing its foreignness. Majestic buildings abutted traditional shops with tiny doors next to flagship stores of international brands. Rows of streetlights leading to a rotund opera house at one end and the imposing Stephansdom Cathedral at the other.

Now Terence was facing the ring road and, beyond it, Karlsplatz. It was after 11:00 p.m. now; he'd lost track of time sitting in the grimy English-language cinema for a double feature. It was a wonder he hadn't fallen asleep. *The Third Man* wasn't the raving excitement promised by the adverts, though *Woman in Gold*, the second film, was more entertaining. And the tub of mixed salty and sweet popcorn he ate in the interval left him hungry.

He turned around and began walking back up Kärtner Straße. As the major shopping street in Vienna, there had to be a restaurant or café open at this hour, even on a Tuesday night. The road was eerily silent, though, at this end. All the lights and fancy shop fronts could not disguise the fundamental feature of life here: it stopped at night. As he approached the centre square with its towering church, Terence was pleased to see a few more souls loitering about. But as he began to pay them more attention, he realised most were tourists with thick American or East European accents, who had, like him, perhaps expected the centre of a major European city to be more active.

He stood for a moment, staring up at the striking cathedral, half covered by protective drapery with adverts for Swarovski and Mozart Chocolates, where flying buttresses and stained glass windows were being repaired. Now and then, someone took a quick photo and moved on. Nearby, a man stared angrily into this mobile phone, cursing Uber for not working in the city. Across from the cathedral, a luxury hotel's enormous sign lit up the starless sky, competing for a bit of the holy limelight. And across from the hotel on a side street, the familiar golden arches of a fast-food chain caught Terence's eye. As he walked in that direction, his stomach growled.

Beneath him, centuries of Roman ruins and gothic tunnels swirled unseen, the history of a city older, almost, than Central Europe itself. And yet, it felt empty in its grandeur. Tomorrow, thousands of people would pass where he now walked. But did any of them care beyond getting to work or snapping a social media photo? Worse yet, would one of them recognise him? 'Isn't that Terrence Matthews, the disgraced English writer?'

Across from the twenty-four-hour chain, a bar with glass doors no bigger than a full-length mirror flickered with the only signs of nightlife. An interracial couple exited, glancing at him as they passed. The smell of beer and wine and sweaty people wafted out as the door slammed shut behind them. Through the window, Terence could see the happy faces of small crowds gathered around tiny tables.

Inside the restaurant with his double cheeseburger and French fries, Terence sat in a booth by the window on the upper floor. Between bites of greasy food, he stared at the bar. It made him remember. Remember the odd night out in bars like this in London, drinking five-pound beers and picking up any guy he wanted, or at least thinking he had it in him to pick them up, though he rarely went through with it. The door of the bar opened again. Out came a man about Terence's age, and this almost made him cry.

II.

Five weeks ago, a lifetime ago, he had been sitting at home in his sleek Canary Wharf flat, reeling over his decision to pull out of the television interview and thinking about the peculiar young man he'd met on the street outside Coffee. Suddenly, the flat was too small to contain Terence. He wanted to go out, to celebrate something. What? Standing up for himself, perhaps. He texted Aaron, an old colleague.

They met an hour later in Soho, Aaron's eyes still red from a day spent reading student essays. 'I don't miss that,' Terence said. He gripped Aaron's hand and pulled him into a bar with rainbow flags hanging over its doors and window casings. 'Let's have one or two?'

The pinks and purples of the strobe lighting, the Formica tables, and the plastic chairs all screamed 'dive,' but it was a place where Terence knew he wouldn't be recognised. Years before, as a new teacher at the academy where Aaron still taught, they had con-fided in each other a mutual dream to one day be full-time 'queer authors.' They had stressed this particular characteristic: both Aaron and Terence wanted to write the defining gay novel, a *Call Me by Your Name* for their generation. It had never been a competition or a rivalry. The two aspiring novelists would meet weekends to write together or to attend literary talks at The British Library. Even when Terence finally hit it big with *Noon at the Louvre*, not a gay novel, but still a major success, Aaron had been nothing but supportive of his pal. They loved each other like brothers.

When they'd ordered their pints, Terence gave Aaron his news.

'Bloody hell,' Aaron said. 'They want to sue you?'

'Wanted to. Past tense. I think Jean-Pierre Mokrani will clean it up.'

'Wow.' Aaron leaned back and scrutinised Terence. 'I always wanted things to go smoothly for you, I hope you know that, mate.'

'I know, but don't worry. J.P. has got as much or more to lose from this as I do.'

'What about your agent or publisher? Have you told them?'

'No can do. My agent would drop me for sure. It's literary suicide, not having an original idea, or worse, being accused of pedalling what amounts to plagiarised work.'

They finished the pints, and Aaron indicated he'd be up for another one. ('I'll just go in hung-over tomorrow.') Terence suggested they move to the bar's basement, which had more of a club atmosphere: DJ, even more intense strobe lighting, and far less seating.

Halfway through his second pint, Terence took to the dance floor. Never a keen dancer, it felt liberating to let go and forget his troubles. Inch-by-inch, he pulled Aaron out with him, and the danced together like they knew each other rather better than they did, or perhaps, like they didn't know each other at all, no more than a histrionic singles meeting for the first time in a seedy London gay club. Their hips pressed to one another established that they would go home together.

For the rest of that second pint and half of another, their hands and feet mingled on the dance floor or under a table in the corner when they weren't dancing. Aaron had many stories, as all teachers do, and this made Terence sentimental.

In the back of an Uber, Aaron fidgeted with his phone, saying at one point that he'd written to his deputy head teacher to say he'd need a substitute tomorrow. Terence found this moving and a bit sweet, even as Aaron leaned across him and dropped his hand onto Terence's crotch.

When they were finally in bed, Aaron got straight to work, quickly undressing and making little fuss over anything else. Terence too was glad to find some relief from his solitude in carnal pleasure. He focussed on their bodies with fierce determination, timing every pull and thrust with precision. The doggedness kept him sober and kept his mind from wandering off to other things. After the deed was done, Aaron fell asleep immediately. Terence's overactive mind was too worked up for sleep. He feared he had ruined their so-called brotherhood, impinged on the friendship they had forged. To him, friendship represented a choice over birthright. It had a special impact because it was not inevitable or forced. But this particular quality of friendship also came with a price tag: you cannot do things to set it off-kilter. Surely, sleeping with a friend counted as one of those things.

The next morning there could be no doubt of the number of drinks they'd had the night before. Terence, not accustomed to drinking anything more than a glass of wine at dinners out, had a splitting headache. Aaron was fine after a black coffee, which they took on the small balcony off the living room.

'It's like a little Manhattan,' Aaron said.

'Is it?' The way the wide spaces of water gave way to small tributaries had always reminded Terence more of Amsterdam or Hong Kong with its skyscrapers on sea level.

'Canary Wharf is nice. Much nicer than where I live,' said Aaron. 'You've got it made, mate.'

Terence didn't respond. It hardly felt right to call someone you'd just slept with 'mate.' From across the room, his phone buzzed.

'I should probably check that,' he said. His heartbeat quickened, expecting to see bad news from Jean-Pierre or, god forbid, his agent. Instead, he had an alert from an unknown number: Missed call.

III.

The service station. Rows on rows of plastic-wrapped foods, cigarette cartons of every brand, soft drinks and beers and crisps packages with large lettering, a man behind a till surrounded by plexiglass and security cameras.

'Got a payphone?' It scared Milo to say too much to the man behind the counter. His bleary, red eyes and gruff beard did little to make you feel welcome, and Milo had the idea the shop assistant might be there more for security reasons and less for customer service.

'You think this is 2014, kid?' The man's voice matched expectations, a harsh, quipping staccato.

'Huh?' Milo swayed back and forth abruptly, needing to use the loo.

'2014. That's when the last telephone box got painted green and turned into a mobile phone charging point.'

'How about a toilet? Got one of those?'

The man pointed to a dark hallway at the back of the shop. 'Gotta buy something to use it.'

'I'll buy something after I'm done, okay?'

The man nodded and diverted his eyes. He stared at a screen behind the till and let out a low guffaw as Milo ran down the back of the shop.

A minute later he was back with a bag of crisps in hand.

'You watch The Chase, kid?' Something about the man's mannerism softened. 'Some funny blokes on here,' he said pointing to the screen, which Milo realised must be a television and not a security camera.

'Don't worry 'bout those,' he said, pointing to the crisps. 'It's on the house.'

'Thanks. You know where I can find a phone?'

'Who you callin'? They local? You can use my phone if so. No calls to China though, kid.'

'Umm, okay, thanks.' Milo opened his rucksack and took out the novel. 'This is the number,' he said, showing it to the man.

'Yeah, it's local all right. Here you go.' He handed his Samsung to Milo and then turned back to the TV.

The line rang. Once, twice, seven times, and then voicemail. 'Umm, hello, Mr, ugh, Terence. This is Milo,'–He looked up to make sure the shop assistant wasn't eavesdropping.–'the guy you met on Bond Street earlier today. You said to call if I needed something. And–'

'Hey, kid, you done with my phone already?'

Clicking the red 'end call' button, Milo handed the phone back. 'Well, thanks,' he said.

On a cold night when you're running away but have no idea where you'll go, London is strange and foreboding place. He'd taken the underground to the stop nearest the park where the funfair had been. It had appeared a more logical choice than the Mayfair area, which he knew got quieter on weeknights. But stepping off the tube into Northern London was like stepping into a wealthy foreign country. Gone were the Ferris wheel and cotton candy stands. In their place were tree-lined streets. Exhaust fumes from Mercedes and Jaguars filled the air. Strangers in designer clothes rushed past in every direction.

Milo stepped back into the underground station and jumped over the turnstile. The few coins in his pocket would not last long, and he couldn't risk using them on train fare. Twelve minutes later, he was in Kings Cross Station.

The terminal teemed with police. Everywhere he looked, there were signs for homeless shelters and food banks next to adverts for fast-food chains and Marks & Spencer. He'd only ever been to Kings Cross once before, as a boy on a school field trip to the British Museum, but it looked so different from the place he remembered. After all day on the streets begging, the journeys to and from the hostel, and the frantic, sweaty run to the service station, Milo was dirty and tired. He began anticipating one of the many police stopping him to ask for ID, which he didn't have, or to —worse yet—place him in child protective services. But no one stopped him, which on second thought was not helpful, since he had given no thought to what to do next or where to go. Could he turn up at a shelter without someone questioning his age or alerting the authorities? And how did it work with seventeen-year-olds? Were they still considered minors? He would turn eighteen soon. Questions he'd never had to ask before because he'd always had a home (well, a bed, at least). Damn Daniel for encouraging him to leave.

Milo continued to walk around the expanse of Kings Cross and then next door in St Pancras Station, pretending to blend in, like he knew where he was going. After he'd covered the station several times over, he walked south, toward the British Museum. He had a vague recollection of where it was and there were signs dotted around irregular streets pointing the way. The wind and the stench of Central London hit him in the face. Although it looked more put together, this was a dirtier and damper place than the area surrounding the hostel, and unexpectedly he felt homesick.

The street in front of the British Museum was quiet. A lone police officer, dressed differently from the ones in the train station, paraded up and down one side of the road, an innocuous security guard. Only one restaurant was open, and it had no customers. The others boarded up each day after the museum closed. Park benches lined the expanse in front of the massive museum complex.

IV.

Milo felt his mind floating back and forth, forth and back as he lay on the thick bench, whose firmness was not unlike that of a hostel bed. And because it was so like the bunk bed he'd grown accustomed to sleeping on, he knew exactly what to do and not to do to get a decent rest. Changing his position, for example from lying on his back to his side, would not make it more comfortable. Moving couldn't still his mind, which was conscious of his predicament even as he slept. He had to place his trust in perseverance and also in an 'I can deal with it tomorrow / one day at a time' attitude. So, he put up no resistance and woke early the next morning to the sounds of big lorries and husky men collecting rubbish from nearby bins.

V.

It had been ten hours since the missed call. Terence was at a loss for what to do. The man to whom the phone number belonged could give him no information, other than to confirm that the boy, Milo, had been in his off-licence the night before and had asked to use his phone. 'Couldn't tell you more, mate.' And now Aaron wanted to go for pizza. They had to eat, didn't they?

Terence was indifferent to the sound of his Stan Smith sneakers shuffling on the floor of the pizzeria. In contrast, the sound of a phone ringing or a text message pinging set his hand to rapidly checking his mobile. Every sound meant anxiety, and every movement was rogue, full of overdone and unwanted emotion. He sat in the tanned pleather pizza shop chair and listened to Aaron's morose chatter. Terence forgot that he should be enjoying this, that they'd just shared a fairly lovely night together, never mind the implications for their friendship. But he had forgotten this in favour of thinking about that boy who had used his number so soon after Terence had given it to him, and who was, he sensed, in trouble.

VI.

Milo gathered his things and walked south toward the river. Longingly, he thought of Daniel and the fun-fair and the taste of sour beer in the cool air. But more to the point, he was hungry. Long queues of peckish tourists filled the cafés and coffee shops around Bloomsbury. But on a more deserted side street, he came to a pastry shop and bought the first cake that caught his eye, an exorbitant use of his meagre funds. The sugar rush at once made him feel better. As Milo ate, licking vanilla frosting off his fingers, he stared at the dubious architecture of this part of London and the demeanour of its people. Leaving the hostel, he'd somehow felt a lot more confident about how all this would play out. Or perhaps he had not thought at all. On his mind now were his mother and Arsenije. Would they come looking for him or report him missing or a runaway to the police? How could he be sure with people so unpredictable? And what about money? He'd have to beg again, only this time for real. And where would he sleep? Park benches every night. Perhaps if he could only try calling Terence Matthews again...

As tired as he was and as cold as it was outside, Milo's spirits lifted to see boys his own age running joyously and haphazardly across the street, chasing each other in what seemed to be a semi-grown game of tag. The smells, the shadows cast by tall buildings, the newly planted trees, they all seemed to speak of fresh life, a promise of future fortune. But they also produced a sense of foreboding. Every shadow cast by a skyscraper was an omen against self-sufficiency; every pleasant smell was followed closely by the stench of rotting food and street people in need of a wash. It was as if two paths lay before him. If he travelled the lighted path, he would walk into a new, refurbished life. But after how much time and how much struggle? He turned onto a long south-facing road. Ahead, the Thames sparkled in the sun's favour.

Suddenly, he stopped. A familiar presence in skinny jeans and a hoodie ambled past and was walking down the pavement ahead with a man by his side. The profile stood out, even from behind, a backside view that perfectly matched the headshot on his book. The duo were preoccupied. The familiar figure seemed more fatigued than Milo remembered, but he still recognised the angle of the man's head, with its faint echo of gentleness.

Milo scurried ahead to catch up. 'Mr Matthews?' he called. The two figures were talking to one another, though Milo couldn't make out what they were saying. 'Mr Matthews—Terence? It's Milo,' he said, pulling at the shadowy figure's sleeve.

It was Milo all right. Terence would have known him anywhere.

SEVEN

I.

Though there was nothing holding him in London, Milo grew more and more anxious as the date approached. Terence, who had been more than kind to give him a place to sleep, had announced he was leaving for Austria. For how long, he couldn't say, but would he, Milo, like to come along? At first, Milo thought it had to be a joke, some kind of test of how far and to what extent he was planning to rely on Terence's hospitality. But the man was true to his word, and the following morning, they were applying for expedited passports.

Two days later, movers showed up and began dismantling Terence's Canary Wharf flat, packing the books into boxes marked 'Storage' and bundling clothes into airtight plastic containers with shipping labels affixed. 'Why the rush?' Milo asked, still unsure how to define their relationship and why Terence would want him to come along, moving to the other side of the continent with someone he barely knew.

'I'm in a bit of trouble here,' Terence said, 'reputation-wise.'

Milo didn't understand.

'Do you watch the news, M?'

Terence had almost immediately taken to calling him M. What a relief to go by something other than Shit-for-brains, Arsenije's preferred nickname for Milo.

'No, not really.' Of all the preoccupations Milo had, keeping current with the news wasn't one of them. He preferred the happy endings in fiction to the grim realities of the real world.

'Well suffice to say I'd be better off away from England for a while. I could use some space.'

'And you really want me to come with you?'

'Have you somewhere else to be?' Terence said with a smile.

Tormented by whatever was happening to Terence, yet unable to do anything about it, Milo hovered, watching the movers dismantle the flat piece-by-piece, until he decided to return to the hostel for what later seemed like a very naïve reason: to say goodbye to his mother.

Scared to tell Terence of his intent, Milo used the last of his pocket money to buy a Zone 3 London Underground return ticket.

Though it had only been a week, there was a smiling, wide-chested woman at the hostel's reception desk, whom he hadn't seen before. Donna (the name on her badge) stepped in front of him as he tried to enter the building without stopping at the desk. 'Can I help you?' she said.

'I, uhh, used to live here,' Milo said, 'and I came back for something.'

'Nobody lives here,' she said, adding, 'It's a hostel.'

'Yeah, I know, but my parents–' He paused, ashamed to have let this slip. '–they were hiring one of the bunks on a long-term basis. If you take me back there,' he pointed down the corridor, 'I can show you which one.'

'Sorry,' Donna said doubtfully, 'but there's nobody else on duty so I've got to remain at the desk.'

Milo had stayed at the hostel long enough to know this wasn't true. The old receptionist was routinely found in the kitchen or out smoking.

'Well,' he said after a frigid pause, 'could you at least tell me if they're still in the same room? Maybe I could leave a note, or wait here till they come out.' This was logical, he thought. If what Daniel had said was true, it would only be a matter of time before Tereza went for a smoke.

Donna nodded and Milo provided his mother and Arsenije's names. It only took her a few moments to check the register. 'Nobody by either of those names here.'

Milo pointed down the corridor as if this was proof of their existence. 'Can you check again?'

She rummaged through the register again, slower this time.

'Ah,' she said, 'here they are. But they checked out five days ago.'

Five days. That was just forty-eight hours after Milo had left. Where could they have gone?

'But that's not on!' He stared at her, willing her to change her answer. 'Did they leave a forwarding address or phone number or something?' But he already knew the answer.

'Like I said, this is a hostel, not a block of flats.'

Milo stood at the reception desk, dismayed and feeling stupid for coming back.

A backpacker entered the building, and Donna grew antsy. 'Anything else, young man?'

'No, thank you. I'll just be going, I guess.'

'Okay, bye, God bless,' she called as he walked out of the hostel for the last time.

II.

The first thing Dagmar ever said to Terence was, 'And who is this?' She was pointing at Milo.

An unusual-looking landlady, Terence thought. Her eyes were too small for her large face, but they were a spectacular brown, a caramel colour he'd never seen on anyone in England. Perhaps these are Central European eyes, he imagined, not knowing what he meant by that. He lowered his own pale blue pupils and said, 'This is my friend. He'll be staying with me.'

Milo had his head down the whole time and only looked up after Terence had put an emphatic full stop on his reply. Dagmar was a short, stout woman, and when Milo bent over and gave her a docile smile, she did not smile back. She looked at him without blinking, narrowed her eyes as if to focus on some feature, and afterwards shook her head. It was neither an affirmative, up and down nod, nor a negative, side-to-side shake, but something in-between, the slightest sign of forced acquiescence. Her gravity made Milo feel self-conscious and unwanted, but he imagined that in the rush of things, Terence hadn't let this lady know a second person would move with him into the flat. The oversight was predictable. For years Milo'd endured the awkwardness of being the odd poor boy amongst the well-off adults. It only hurt now because Terence was a witness.

'Come through for tea,' she said. 'We can do the paperwork, too.'

Her thick enunciation lent itself to sliding over all the syllables that should have been punctuated, a quality that reminded Milo of Arsenije and made him doubt this woman more.

A young lady about eighteen or nineteen sat at Dagmar's kitchen table. As they entered the room, she stood to greet them. Though considerably taller and with smoother skin, it was clear she was the landlady's daughter. 'I'm Katrin,' she said with an English dialect so perfect it made both Terence, the world traveller, and Milo feel at ease and less like foreigners. Katrin made a pot of tea as Terence and Dagmar started on the papers.

When Katrin returned to the table with a tray of mugs, a warmness radiated from her, sending a ripple up Milo as he was reminded of his mother in better times. This made conversation easy. As the two adults got on with business, Milo and Katrin played the familiar game of casual greeting and safe small talk indicative of young people who have just met. If not for Katrin, Milo might have discovered nothing more about the building or its landlady, topics which now interested him purely because Katrin brought them up.

'And your mum, she's from Austria?'

'Yes, but her parents were wealthy Czechs. They left her this building. It was in a dire state until we renovated it.'

'*You* renovated it?'

'I was ten, but I helped.' She smiled for the first time, and Milo saw her yellowing teeth. They betrayed her. Everything else about this girl was put-together, but those teeth signalled a kind of personal neglect. *Drugs*, he thought, remembering the look of some of the beggars he'd seen in London.

'Well anyway,' she said after a pause, 'I'm glad we have new tenants now. That will be good for her.'

'And I hope I will see you around,' Milo said, with rather too much caution, but it had been a long time since he'd made a female friend.

She gave him a flirtatious smile. 'You will, now and again.'

Milo watched Terence and Dagmar fold up the papers and rise from the table. 'I'll you show to the flat,' Dagmar said and motioned them along. To his disappointment, Katrin stayed behind.

'See you around,' Katrin said, flashing her awful teeth again.

But she is beautiful, anyway, Milo thought.

III.

The sparsely furnished flat comprised two rooms connected by a door, either of which could be a living room or bedroom, a tiny kitchen with space for a cafe-style table and two chairs, and a shower room. The builders had shoved a water closet behind a door in one corner of the kitchen. The layout presented an immediate problem Terence hadn't anticipated: sleeping arrangements. In fact, he'd done very little in the way of logical thinking in the past week. From the one-night stand with Aaron to Milo sleeping on his sofa and learning of the boy's story to now relocating the two of them here, to Vienna, it had all happened so quickly and almost robotically. He had done it all step-by-step without concern for the bigger picture or the future consequences, an impetuousness he had never known before and yet embraced.

Perhaps as a way to contemplate worst outcomes or as a way to avert them, Terence considered his options. Milo could sleep on the sofa; that would be easiest. Or perhaps they'd get two twin beds and bunk up like college roommates. A memory of Jean-Pierre. No, the sofa then. Because who was he kidding? Milo was seventeen, half his age. Possibly not even gay. Someone lost and in need of shelter. Was it wrong to offer that under the guise of quid pro quo? He could already foresee hollow evenings in dead cold Austria, nights spent alone with Milo's young flesh just barely out of reach. Long days spent reading and writing and trying to recover his reputation, however one does that, while Milo did what? Could the boy find work or take a language class or...?

Terence stopped himself, knowing by inverse logic that all these doubts presumed that his present-day happiness would evaporate. But that wasn't so, not yet. He had to be hopeful, and to back that up with the craving he felt fiercely. So fierce that he imagined even Dagmar, that woman with her knowing scowl and hollow pleasantry, could guess how completely smitten he was with Milo. But did Milo see it?

'I'm afraid there's only one bed in here,' Terence said, looking down sheepishly and trying to pass it off as embarrassment for the oversight. When Milo said nothing, Terence looked around the room, pretending to search for sudden options to appear. 'Well, there's the sofa,' he said at last, sounding reluctant.

'Well, I'm fine with anywhere,' Milo said, unfazed. 'I still can't believe I'm here. I mean only last week I was sleeping on a park bench.'

Terence sighed and told him for the tenth time in half as many days that there was no need to say thank you or even to lament the past. He couldn't extricate Milo's appreciation from his own feelings, which had crept up on him like a thief. And now, Terence determined to show he was not uncomfortable with this arrangement, perhaps even a little glad for it.

'You decide then.' It felt safe to leave it at that.

Things were happening so fast for Milo that he would have gone along with anything at this point. Terence was acting strangely, but whether this was jet lag or stress or anxiety at the situation, Milo couldn't say. It reminded him of Daniel, a transiency that lent itself to such whims in older men. Milo didn't know for sure, but he thought Daniel and Terence only a few years apart in age. To his mind, Terence's plain wealth compared to Daniel's had more to do with class upbringing than age, and yet he sensed himself feeling for Terence what he'd felt for Daniel, or at least something approximating it. It had been a hundred times easier to open up to Terence, perhaps because he had already done it with Daniel. But there was more to it than that. He remembered the intimacy he shared with Daniel, the kiss and the surrounding euphoria. He wanted it again, now, with Terence. But he remembered Johnny, and he was scared. He could no longer shun the past; it had come crawling out of its grave like a zombie that just wouldn't die.

'The couch, I guess,' said Milo. At once, he could see the disappointment on Terence's face and regretted saying it. Hadn't he promised himself that he would try to trust kind people?

'Or, well, we could share the bed, maybe,' Milo ventured. But changing his mind did not produce a change in feeling. Still, he felt regret. He could not take advantage of Terence this way. Now Terence would feel obliged to say yes, out of pity. Or worse, he'd say 'Suit yourself' or 'I suppose so'. Indecisive, forced answers.

Terence bent his head to one side. Had he heard correctly or was this fanciful thinking?

'Only maybe,' Milo added, 'it's not a good idea?'

'It's a wonderful idea,' Terence said. In that packed, dark flat with one bed, the words flowed out, cementing the roles that he and Milo seemed destined to play in this foreign land.

EIGHT

I.

For all his early apprehension, Terence found himself so preoccupied in Vienna that he hardly noticed the days pass, until at the McDonald's after the cinema, he saw something in the bar-goers the street opposite that reminded him of home and of the difficulties Austria presented. He wondered if he could even think of London as home now. He'd spent so much effort to block out that city. Days passed changelessly and almost effortlessly. His German began to improve. *Hallo, sprechen Sie englisch? Ich spreche ein bisschen deutsch.*

Autumn days were turning to winter nights, the crisp air and crunch of leaves on cobblestones. For Terence and Milo, it was like an extended holiday.

Everything was fun and made them laugh or filled them with interest, a desire to know and read more. Even the small flat felt like part of the adventure, more like a large hotel room than a *Wohnung*. Sometimes, just as the sun was setting, they could look out of the bay window and see the sky splayed in blues and purples and magentas. *Erzähl mir eine Geschichte*. Tell me a story, Terence would say, challenging Milo to practice his German.

Ich kann noch nicht genug deutsch, he'd reply, explaining 'I don't know enough.'

'That's because you're only going to lessons once a week,' Terence had said. But, in those early days, they hadn't needed words. So attuned to each other's moods that the one could set off the other just by smiling a little awkwardly or raising an eyebrow askew. A fit of laughter would follow, and Milo invariably would suggest they watch any one of his new favourite movies –Mrs Doubtfire, Sister Act, Miss Congeniality–90s and 2000s American films he'd never watched as kid or had seen so long ago that he'd forgotten their plots.

Their diets began to suffer, too, or Terence's did. (Milo's, he reckoned, had never been that healthy to begin with.) The tiny kitchen cupboards stored cereal, milk, ramen noodles, and not much else. Terence had seen fit to take Milo to a general practitioner for a physical, the first one he'd had as a teenager. He was promptly prescribed a multivitamin he took whenever he could remember, which wasn't every day. Movies, sunsets, junk food, city tours. Though they slept in the same bed, they never touched. Still, each day was something to be treasured. Time passed this way for a month.

II.

But then, shortly after his eighteenth birthday (celebrated with schnitzel and Diet Coke), Milo ran into Dagmar, the landlady, in the corridor.

'You have weed?' she asked.

'Sorry?' Her question startled Milo. It was the first time he had run into Dagmar since they had moved in. She looked a little less intimidating in the bright of day than she had in his jet-lagged state.

'There have been complaints,' she said, 'from others in the building saying they can smell marijuana. I've never smelt it myself though.'

'Oh,' Milo took a cautious step forward. 'It's not us.' He could see her face soften a bit as though she'd never seriously suspected him anyway, but he added, just to be sure: 'I've never even seen marijuana.'

'Figures,' Dagmar said, rubbing her chin. 'You don't look the type.'

'Oh. Okay.' He felt a heaviness in his chest that he thought, at first, was caused by her abruptness, but later realised was because of the question he was about to ask.

'Your daughter,' he began, guarded, 'Katrin. Is she around?' This was not exactly the question he had in mind, but it was difficult to say precisely what he wanted. He'd thought of Katrin, that girl with the strange name and perfect accent, off and on since that first day. He remembered wandering from room to tiny room in their flat just minutes after meeting her trying to capture what he'd felt and what he'd been doing and how he'd been acting when they first saw each other. First Daniel, then Terence, then Katrin, then Terence again—they all existed for him on a kind of spectrum of similar feelings, almost interchangeable emotions. Was this because he hadn't had the potential for even a friend for so long, he wondered, or was this how love felt? And if so, what did it mean to want love from all three of them?

'Katrin is in school,' Dagmar said. She had a questioning look in her eyes, clouds of grey rolled over brown pupils.

'Oh, right, it's Tuesday.' He had thought Katrin was older. Too old for school anyway, but maybe she went to the local university. Or maybe girls aged differently here, appearing wiser and more mature than their English counterparts.

'Not because it's Tuesday,' Dagmar said. She gave a terse nod, a 'stupid kid' look all too familiar to Milo. 'She's away. At boarding school. Switzerland.'

With her condescending look, Milo had all but tuned out. But those three phrases in Dagmar's dark, matter-of-fact voice stung him with the same intensity as Daniel's leaving had done.

'But she was just here, a few weeks ago, in your kitchen.' Milo said this as if he had to remind her of the facts.

'End of summer break. They don't start until mid-September there.' Dagmar took a step forward. It was clear she had other things to do.

Milo tugged at her sleeve, a gesture at once aggressive and childlike. It was the same way he had tugged at Terence's hoody on the street in London. 'But when will she be back?'

'Christmas break, child,' Dagmar said, patting him on the back. It was a show of affection that surprised them both.

III.

Terence put his palm on his chest. 'Her?' he said. 'Total co-ed.' He paused, surprised by the juvenile way he'd spoken. He hadn't thought he had it in him to regress to phrases like 'co-ed.' These were the kind of words he'd always felt better suited to white girls from Chelsea and the rich French of Jean-Pierre's ilk, people with too much money and too little class.

'Oh, well,' Milo said, surprised at the fierceness, though maybe he shouldn't have been. 'I just wondered about her, that's all.' It struck him that he'd upset Terence, that in enquiring about the girl and consequently bringing her up to Terence, he'd disturbed the invisible balance of their domestic life. The happy existence they'd had for the past month now seemed precarious, and he felt guilty for it.

'You ought to be careful,' said Terence. 'Girls like that are trouble. They lead you on and leave you dry. And you won't even know what you're in for.'

'Oh,' Milo said. None of this made any sense to him, nor did Terence's warnings sound like reasons to dislike someone he'd only spent a matter of minutes with. Milo shifted restlessly. They were standing by the bay window. 'Really! What do you *really* think about her?' he blurted out.

'What?!' Terence's tone was curious, not angry or sarcastic, even Milo could hear that. But a delicate thread in the fabric of their domesticity unravelled.

'Forget it,' Milo said. He turned and walked to the bedroom, slamming the door behind him.

Terence opened the window and let the breeze from the street below hit him in the face. He wondered what had made him so harsh on Milo, besides the obvious: that he was slowly, surely falling for this boy. That girl, or indeed any girl or boy, represented a challenge to those feelings. And that Milo had brought it up so casually ('She's away until December, so maybe I'll never get to know her.') showed just how much of a gap there was between where Terence wanted things to be and what Milo wanted.

Before tonight, he had been hopeful. It was a hope fuelled by their willingness to go with the flow, to take each day as it came. They'd quickly fallen into a routine, and it felt almost inspired. Behind that hope was a thirst, or maybe even a touch of lust, that was intense precisely because it was taboo and just out of touch. Now, nothing would come of it. Terence had lost Milo to the invisible presence of the literal 'girl next door,' not that he could logically place blame. She would be better for Milo in lots of ways, he imagined, age not the least of it. But maybe the problem was not with this girl or with Milo, but with his own inability to state his desires directly.

Terence didn't mind Milo knowing he had feelings for him. In fact, he wanted Milo to know. *But boys like Milo do not understand about these things*, he thought. Who does at that age? And they've no idea of the lengths grown men go to disguise their feelings. He wanted to say, 'Let's do this, let's just see where it goes, crazy as it is.' What he didn't want was to show his weakness.

Inside the bedroom, the door remained closed. Milo sat on a carpet beside the bed. It would make sense, he knew, to lie on the bed or to sulk in the rattan chair in the corner, but there was something soothing about the hard coolness of the floor. Almost as soon as he'd slammed the door, he'd regretted his actions, re-gretted bringing the whole goddamned thing up. 'I just wondered about her.' A silly, childlike thing to say when he'd been trying so hard since they arrived in Vienna to act like a man. He had snapped at Terence, and rather than snap back, as Milo had expected—as almost everyone he'd ever known would have done—Terence grew calm, practically tormented.

The door opened. To ward off Terence's gaze, Milo looked elsewhere and tried to act distracted. He wanted some sympathy; he wanted Terence to ask why he'd stormed in here, and he wanted that man to worry that he could lose what they had, or might have. But then again, Milo wanted to be left alone. He'd not been by himself for any amount of time in weeks. Now this pretend indifference to Terence played at a double meaning: leave me alone and comfort me.

'Pizza?' Terence repeated as though snapping a finger to get Milo's attention. 'I asked if you want pizza for dinner? I'll order it.'

'You don't have to get me anything,' Milo responded.

'It's dinner. So, it's for both of us.'

The hairs on Milo's arms glistened with sweat. He knew he was being unreasonable. He could easily have said 'yes,' accepting the olive branch Terence extended, but he was unable to extricate himself from the floor. Physically glued to the rug, he conveyed the impression he was more intent on going down this slope than he was grateful for the attention.

Terence asked again. Milo insisted he was fine, adding he'd make something for himself later. It was a last-ditch effort at exerting independence.

Then it happened, as Milo feared.

'Suit yourself,' Terence said. He might as well have said 'Fuck it,' for that's how Milo heard it. The words were laced with a tedium bordering on resignation or boredom. Milo couldn't be sure which, and he instantly repressed his stubbornness as a result.

'What kind of pizza?' A fumbled attempt to make time go back several seconds.

'Oh, just relax. I'll order it.' Exasperation festered in Terence's voice as he left the room.

As he searched online for pizza delivery joints, he wondered if this affected imperviousness was Milo's way, not of pushing people away or of trying to defuse the situation, but of going through the motions of feigned dismissal, like a dog whose bark is worse than his bite, a puppy who just wants to be cuddled.

Terence had spent little time considering Milo's past. To say it had been traumatic was a gross simplification, but everyone's childhood is traumatic. The peculiar nature of his upbringing, though, had to explain some of this behaviour, Terence thought. Everything about him got magnified and muddled, and for someone whose only structure comprised days spent on pavements begging for change, this made sense. To question Milo's behaviour was, when seen through this lens, almost unfair. What could Milo know of commitment or discretion? Even his way of speaking and his peculiar, innocent expressions were telling. They required instant understanding and self-less empathy, things no reasoned adult with life exper-ience ever rationally expects. Milo held nothing back, concealed no part of his thought process, or so Terence imagined. But the drawback of this candour was that his innocence could come off as disrespectful and hurtful. Underneath all this agitated behaviour, starting with that girl Katrin and ending with this sulking tantrum, was a boy just trying to make sense of the world. And aren't we all?

IV.

'I have to work,' Terence said. He hadn't picked up a pen or opened his laptop in a month.

He felt pensive and weary walking through the empty streets around their flat. *What is wrong with me?* he thought. *Why do I hold it against Milo that his old life still haunts him? It wasn't even so long ago, only a matter of weeks. This was normal behaviour, perhaps even a type of separation anxiety. Still...*

When he came to the city centre, its oppressive buildings and throngs of tourists, the sadness only deepened. He had assumed getting out of the flat, giving Milo space and himself some time to write would ease the tension of the night before, but now a certain melancholy littered the air and invaded his psyche.

Around him, people were smiling and happy, taking selfies and sitting for coffees at traditional cafés.

Neither a chain coffee shop nor a handful of restaurants on the main square looked like suitable places to work. He hoped to stumble on an Austrian version of Coffee, just as quaint as its Mayfair predecessor but perhaps with wood panelling and a barista in lederhosen. Instead, he settled for a no-brand teahouse where two people sat working on their computers. At least he could try to fit in there.

It ought to have been simple enough to pick up the unfinished manuscript he'd been working on in London, but he met the screen with a blank stare. The cursor blinked incessantly, as did his train of thought. It was only the rankest luck he had mollified Milo so easily. With pizza of all things. But it seemed to Terence that there was an unshakeable menace behind Milo's actions. Terence reminded himself, again, of the boy's circumstances. And why did he insist on thinking of Milo as a boy, a small creature in need of comfort?

Yet, perversely, this made him long to know Milo more and to care for him in unspeakable ways. Sitting in the teahouse with its bland décor, he envisaged their flat as a gilded hideaway. The worry and uncertainty of last night he now fantasised as a mysterious, romantic period drama between the professorial and the young manservant. The fantasy brought delight and terror. But though he thought of the flat as a refuge, he also knew instinctively that they could not hole up forever. One of the first things they'd done on arriving in Austria was to get Milo a mobile phone, one of those cheap plastic models designed for students and people on a budget. Though he'd had no cause to use it before, Terence rang Milo up. They'd meet at six, he said. A drink and dinner.

In a booth at the back of the café, Terence said, 'I thought it would be nice to get to know each other better,' laying out his intentions for the evening like an academic spelling out his thesis statement.

Milo wondered whether this was Terence's way with everyone. With, for example, that man he'd been spotted with near the Thames, a man who'd Terence brushed off as 'just an old colleague,' putting exaggerated emphasis on *just*. Terence didn't seem to mind silence or awkward pauses, and Milo could appreciate this, having spent much time in the silent shadows of the street, but Terence's lukewarm, devil-may-care form was too direct, too expectant. Milo braced himself before taking the plunge. 'We've spent every day together for the past month.'

'How much do we really know of one another, though?'

Terence was leaning over the table. *Was he really serious?* Milo thought. *He already knows so much. So much.*

For a moment, Terence thought he caught a well-grounded nod. Or was he imagining things? 'Tell me about your yourself,' he suggested.

'Like what?' said Milo in the self-mocking, almost rebellious tenor of the night before.

'Anything at all.' Terence leaned back in his chair.

Milo acted as if this were some kind of game. 'Well, there's not much to say. You already know everything.'

'No one can know everything about someone else.' It was a vague philosophical line, something said to keep himself from sounding annoyed.

'Not much to say,' Milo repeated. He didn't know why there was so little to say. *Because I've already told this guy more than I've told anyone before, even Daniel? And I went through it all so quickly because I'm only a shadow now of what I was before. I'm only now figuring it out. And why can't he see this?* As Milo argued with himself, he also knew that someone had to break the silence. 'Well, I like paintings,' he offered.

'Oh! Which artists? Any paintings in particular?'

'There's one...' Milo lowered his head, more flustered than ever. He'd felt the words slip from his mouth, a half-lie met with anticipation.

Terence's gaze glued onto him.

'Self-portrait by Munch.'

'Love Munch,' Terence said. There was no challenge in his words, no intended unspoken message, still he could detect the flutter of frustration in his young companion. 'Which one?'

A question met with a blank stare.

Was Milo being difficult just as they'd broken the ice? 'Which self-portrait, I mean?'

It had not occurred to Milo that an artist could or would produce more than one famous self-portrait. He had thought if Daniel knew of the painting, then Terence, who was by the looks of it culturally superior, would instantly know it, too. 'Do you always ask people to talk about themselves?' he quipped, desperate to change the line of enquiry.

Terence only smiled, nonplussed until Milo gave in.

'Well, the one with the cigarette,' said Milo.

'Ah, the 1895 self-portrait,' Terence said. 'It's one of my favourites.'

And again, the intensity of his stare. *Should I stare back?* Milo considered. Perhaps it wasn't so much the glare but the man who intimidated him. 'Homeless' Milo was used to people staring. But those were people with no interest in him beyond their temporary distraction. Terence, though, had a stare that could overwhelm you, a stare that could strangle a conversation and promise intimacy before its time. It was as though he were coaxing you into playing Truth or Dare, forcing you to admit your insecurities.

'Do you always stare like this?' It came out harshly, more harshly than Milo had intended. A moment more under that gaze, though, and he'd have gone crazy. He wanted to say, 'I don't know myself; I don't know what I want or what I'm doing here.' But what would happen then? He could find himself on the streets again, only this time in a foreign country and with no one to call, not even a Terence.

'What a strange thing to say.' Terence leaned over the table again as if to demonstrate that his stare could be even closer and more intense.

'*I'm* strange?' The preoccupation in Milo's voice made plain the inward turning of the question.

'This is silly,' Terence said.

Revelling in the space for quiet consideration, Milo let a moment pass. 'Silly because we're not sleeping together?' It seemed to come from outside him, and yet there it was. The inconvenient truth. But the words stung like an insect, the pain increasing as its poison spread through the blood vessels, deep into the parts that had been harmed. They were both staring at the floor now.

'That had occurred to me,' Terence said. He pretended not to be startled.

Milo eased his coolness with a wry smile to mean *I thought so*.

A silence sat between them as quickly as thunder trembles lightning. When they both refused to avert their stares or to move their mouths, it was clear they had wished for the same thing and yet had also wished for it never to be brought up.

'Well, never mind,' Milo said at last. He forced himself to smile. It was a smile both years ahead of him in maturity and woefully ignorant of how love works. There was something modest and helpless in his voice.

Terence paid the bill, and they walked home in silence. He knew better, didn't he? Suddenly the distance between them was wider than the gap in their ages.

V.

'Wake up!'

The voice echoed in Terence's head as the remnants of a dream.

'Hey, Tom, wake up!' Milo shook him.

'What time is it?'

It was 10:30. Terence's eyes creaked open. Milo stood at the edge of the bed, fully dressed down to the sneakers Terence gave him from a pile of ones he no longer wore.

Through the haze of sleep, Terence tried to make out if Milo was in trouble. 'What is it, M?'

'Let's go out for lunch,' he said. And then reconsidering his position, he added: 'Can we go out, please? I know a cool place.'

Twenty minutes later, they were out the door, and after another ten on the train, they alighted at a stop to the north of the city centre.

'Where are we, M?'

'I passed by here on the way to German class last week,' he said. The innocent smile plastered on his face morphed into a sign of his eagerness for approval. 'It's this way.' Milo took Terence by the hand and led him down a deserted street, an excited child leading a reluctant adult.

Terence wanted to know two things: first, how Milo could have stumbled on this road, nowhere near the German school; and second, what had come over Milo since last night to put him in this pleasant mood? But before Terence could ask, they came to a quaint diner with a brick facade and an old wooden door. Ashy-grey windows concealed all but the faintest trace of lights hanging over window seats. A faded sign said 'Otto's' in archaic script.

Otto's Restaurant was a lonely, unloved place. 'Like something out of a dilapidated *The Sound of Music* set,' Terence said.

'Well, let's have something,' Milo said.

'Yes, okay.' Terence contrived to play along.

They sat in one of the lighted tables near a front window. The server had to be over sixty, and wore a pink apron so faded that it reminded one of Pepto-Bismol. She brought a menu and two glasses of tap water. The menu was all in German and, though they'd both been in lessons, they looked at it stumped over the differences between Holsteiner Schnitzel, Wiener Schnitzel, and Putenschnitzel. '*Entschuldigung, haben Sie ein englisches Menü?*' Terence asked. The woman in pink growled.

'Gotta go to the toilet,' Milo said. 'You decide for us.'

Through the cracks in the window frosting, Terence could see the outline of an abandoned factory building opposite. So immersed in thought, he'd not noticed it earlier. He consulted the menu again and settled on the dish of the day, an easy and reliable choice. That done, he again looked out the window. Just then, a few young men exited the factory. It was difficult to make out their precise number or age from behind the frosting. No sooner had they exited did they scurry off in different directions. *Squatters*, thought Terence.

Milo returned, sat down, and downed the water in one go.

'So, what's it going to be?'

Terence pointed to the daily offer. He put his elbows on the table and leaned into a serious position. 'I would have never found this place without you,' he said.

Milo sat still.

Say something, Terence thought. *Ask me why I'm staring at you. Tell me what you know about this random street. Why did you bring me here?* Terence sat back in his seat and removed his elbows from the table.

Chills shot through Milo as though he were terribly cold even though a fire burned in a wood stove not ten feet away.

'I love days like this,' Terence said to make conversation.

Milo crossed his arms and stared through the cracks in the frosting.

'Reminds me of Sunday mornings spent in the Docklands at one of the restaurants that line the canals.' said Terence. He paused, hoping for a response. 'I used to go there sometimes with friends.'

'With that guy? The one I found you with that day.'

'So that's what this is all about?'

Milo fiddled with a sugar packet. 'No, not exactly.'

For a change, it felt like Milo's responsibility to say the next thing, a relief to Terence. And yet it was Terence who functioned like a snake who has just shed its skin: iridescent and permeable.

'Well, I think I like days like this, too,' Milo said, meaning being there with Terence, being in a place he had discovered first and then shared, letting him decide what they ate. He liked all of this.

'So, you're not upset?'

'I'm not upset.'

'Because if it's any consolation, that guy was, or is, just a friend, an old colleague of mine from when I was a teacher.'

'You were a teacher?'

Terence nodded. *Oh, there are so many things you don't know about me, Milo.* 'Munch,' he said, suddenly as if he'd just thought of the artist.

Milo's neutral face turned into the sky at sunset. Tan and cream flesh grew pink and blue.

'The self-portrait with a cigarette. It's not such a sad picture when you compare it to his other famous self-portrait. Do you know it?'

Milo said he didn't and that he enjoyed being taught.

'*Self-Portrait in Hell*. Tells you something about how he saw himself, in his own private hell. But he's not there as a helpless victim. Munch stands upright and proud, totally aware of his own hell but deciding not to give in to it.'

It shook Milo. The trembling in his hands grew, and he raised one hand and offered it up in the space between them. He grabbed Terence's arm and pulled him across the table. He kissed him on the lips, a gentle sweet salute that lingered for a few moments.

Distracted by the kiss, Terence hastened to pay the bill. They hurried to catch the train. They rode the lift to their flat. Mechanical actions in anticipation of the touch to come.

Inside, the bed was suddenly built for two acting as one, not simply two sharing a space. Terence touched Milo's thigh, hip connected to hip, belly to belly. *What if I told him*, Terence thought, *that I know this is crazy, but I don't care? All we need is a little practice. The smell of your skin on my skin and on these sheets. You and me, Milo.*

Milo didn't dare move too much, letting Terence take the lead. He became conscious of his partner's creating and sought to mimic it, matching rhythm for rhythm, replicating the same moans and groans. A pupil copying his teacher.

And then it was over, and Milo latched on to never daring this again. His resolve was gone. He studied the ceiling. He was not sorry it had happened, but he was no longer committed to it. Now that it had happened, it was done. *What now?* he thought. *Do we hold hands or shower or...?*

'You're amazing, kid,' Terence said, leaning in to hold Milo.

Milo rolled over on his side. 'Don't call me kid.'

Terence cuddled him. Milo's cold skin trickled with sweat.

VI.

'It's difficult to know what to say after,' Milo confessed.

Terence rubbed his eyes. He wasn't expecting this. 'You don't have to say anything.'

Scarcely a week had passed, and though Milo had had no thought of sleeping with Terence a second time, somehow he was lying there staring at the ceiling again.

Was this how it would always be? They both wondered. Neither said a word.

Milo reached for a ragged, off-white wife beater. Slipping it over his head, he said: 'Dagmar says Katrin will be back in a few weeks on winter break. Apparently, they get a whole month off.'

Not this again. Terence sighed and pulled on his own shirt, which he'd thrown on the floor beside the bed. 'You've been speaking to Dagmar?'

'Well, only when I pass her in the hall.' Something in the set of his shoulders and the crook of his back suggested this wasn't true.

'You have German in an hour,' Terence said. 'Better get ready. And do you have money for the train? I can give you some, otherwise.'

'I've got enough.' Milo took off the undershirt and began rummaging through the dresser for clean clothes. 'Well, anyway Dagmar says they have a big Christmas party every year, and we're invited.'

Terence raised his eyebrows. 'Our landlady doesn't seem like the kind of person who would host a party.'

'Well, yeah, I know that.'

Terence kept silent, trying to figure out what this meant.

'That's why we should go,' Milo added.

Or is it because of the girl? Terence thought. 'Okay, let's see.'

'What do you mean, "Let's see."?'

Milo stood naked over Terence, who was prostrate on the bed.

'I mean I'll find out the details, and we'll decide if we're going.'

'I'll go if I want to go. You can't tell me what to do.' Milo's face lit up like fine porcelain.

Terence took Milo by the hands. 'Okay, calm down.'

Milo jerked away. 'Fuck you. I don't need to calm down.'

'Sit down!' The shout frightened both of them.

'You don't really know her,' Milo said, breathless and a little desperate.

'Who? Who don't I know?' Though he knew the answer.

'Katrin. You don't even know her, and you judge her like... like—'. Milo stopped, unsure of where to take this.

'You don't know her either, M.'

'Fuck off.' Milo scampered away. A few moments later, the sound of the water running in the shower shattered the silence he left in his wake.

VII.

Instead of taking the train, Milo walked to clear his head. It was a clammy autumn day. Darks clouds overhead threatened to burst at any moment, and he had no umbrella. He marvelled at the fact that he cared about getting wet, that the thought of not carrying an umbrella had even crossed his mind. That would never have been a consideration in Britain. There, he welcomed rainy days: people were more generous when it rained. Moving to Austria (or was it moving in with Tom?) made it feel like he'd been transported from Kansas to Munchkin Land. Now everything was in colour, but gone was the innocence of not carrying any real responsibility. Things here were old and historic and rather beautiful, but they also teemed with anxiety. It was difficult for Milo to separate the city from the circumstances. Terence always seemed to be expecting something of him.

His phone jingled in his pocket. Earlier, he had thought of ringing Terence a dozen times, but embarrassment had kept him from it. Instead, Milo resorted to anger, the one emotion that scared him most. It was the emotion his mother and Arsenije and all the annoyed pedestrians of his former 'career' always fell back on. Milo knew now he was no better than they were. Often at night, back in the hostel and even when he was younger, he would lull himself to sleep by thinking of himself on a podium, a real Olympic-style platform where he was on the gold medal step, receiving some future reward for endurance or good-naturedness and long suffering. That was one thing that gave him hope.

At last the first trickle of rain fell as he turned into the narrow, empty alleyway. Across the road, Otto's appeared to be closed. Milo rapped on the door of the factory building three long times followed by one short knock. It was the code he'd been given. A man he didn't recognise answered.

'Uhm, hello? Is Tobias here? He told me to meet him–'

'*Deutsch sprechen!*'

Milo tried clumsily to mutter the same sentence in German.

'*Hier,*' the man said, opening the door and pointing down a dark and damp hallway.

The next thing Milo would remember was how different the light had become–bright and warm–and he was kneeling beside the guy he recognised as Tobias. Beside him a puddle of vomit wreaked fresh.

Milo felt rotten, and he smelled it too; his own odour made him want to puke again. 'What did you do to me, man?'

Tobias was the other new kid in German class, a transplant from the U.S. whose mother was Austrian. He'd never bothered learning the language until his father took a job at the United Nations, moving the family to Vienna.

'Didn't do shit, bro. You said you wanted to try it.'

Milo felt a sting at the back of his eyes. 'You said we could skip class, drink beers, and hang out.' He stood up by leaning on Tobias for support. His legs wobbled beneath him.

'What'd you give me? That wasn't beer.'

'Was too, bro. Laced with coke.'

'Holy fuck!' Gathering all his strength, a paltry amount in this state, Milo pushed Tobias forward. He hardly moved. He had known better than to try beer again. The sudden thought of Daniel made him want to cry. 'And what time is it?' Through the broken glass window panes, the sun sat high in the sky. Two girls, around sixteen, and a man in his early twenties came into the space and sat in dilapidated sofas lining the perimeter around a makeshift fire pit. In the corner, a tiny grey mouse scurried across and into an opening in the floorboards.

'Hey, rough one last night, eh?' One of the girls had a thick accent. She and the other two giggled and picked up a bong sitting near the fire.

'Oh my god, is it tomorrow?' Sweat rolled down Milo's arms at the realisation that he had been there overnight. Frantically, he patted down his pockets. 'Where's my phone, Tobias? Where's my coat?'

'This yours?' A stranger held up Terence's Canada Goose. Milo had borrowed the coat days before. Snatching it, he turned back to Tobias. 'My phone?'

The punch hit with such force that Tobias scarcely had time to shake his head. No sooner was it done, Milo ran from the room and onto the street, stopping only after he was confident no one had followed him. *You're a violent fucker*, he thought. *Just as you always knew you'd be.*

To his relief, his wallet (which anyway was one of Terence's old ones and contained nothing but two five-euro notes and Dagmar's business card) and keys were still in the inner coat pocket. He bought a train ticket and braced himself for the inevitable talk with Terence.

VIII.

Terence woke exhausted. It was a wonder he had slept at all. For the last two or three weeks, Milo hadn't come straight home after his German class, always saying he'd stayed late to study, never mentioning any details. So, Terence hadn't immediately worried when dinnertime rolled around and he still wasn't back, especially considering their argument. By 9:00, Terence resolved to send a text, even if this made him appear fatherly. No response, only the double-blue check mark to show the message had been read. An hour later, with still no response, Terence couldn't stop fuming about Milo's passive aggressiveness. Here was a young person, someone by who all accounts had a nonexistent social life, and now in a strange country, who knew what he'd gotten up to. A phone call, then. He talked himself into this at 10:30 p.m. Voicemail. 'Where are you, Milo?'

At 9:30 the next morning, the door creaked open. Terence leapt from the sofa and ran the short way to the corridor, stopping midway. What was he to do? Throw his arms around Milo? Slap him across the face? Milo looked to be in one piece, and it would serve him right. But no, that was not the solution. Terence stood there silently, willing his face neutral.

Milo closed his eyes and felt himself being lifted out of his body, floating like a hot-air balloon. He removed the coat and hung it on a peg. Still, Terence did not move. Milo closed his eyes again and tried to picture the Munch self-portrait, the one with the cigarette, but all he could conjure was an image of himself in hell. But not proud like the artist. No, very defeated and ashamed.

'I'm sorry,' Milo said, opening his eyes.

Terence shrugged and let some colour onto his face. 'Where were you?'

'With a friend.'

The casualness frightened Terence beyond anything he had experienced in all the time waiting on Milo to come home. He found himself pleading. 'What "friend"?'

'From German class, but they stole my phone.'

'Oh.' There was something left unsaid, but Terence took a step forward and reached out his arms. 'You reek,' he said, 'like alcohol and piss.'

Milo had been smiling happily in the embrace. Now, he sobered. 'I threw up. Drank too much.'

'Oh,' Terence said after a brief pause.

'Well, I didn't want to.'

'What do you mean, you "didn't want to"?'

'I didn't want to,' he repeated.

Terence looked away. This was going nowhere. 'All right, go clean up. We'll deal with it later.'

'Can it. There's nothing to deal with.'

Palpable panic overtook Terence. He had the sense of losing blood; his head throbbed. 'What are you saying?'

'Never mind,' Milo jabbered. He walked past, head down.

IX.

Milo left in the afternoon. 'Going out,' he said before Terence could object. That night, Milo came back with take-away from the sketchy Chinese restaurant on the corner. Terence had made it a point to avoid the place, redolent as it was of fried dough and MSG. But there was something sweet in the gesture, especially the extra order of prawn crisps for sharing.

'So...,' Terence said. Milo was in the kitchen washing up the cutlery.

Milo smiled innocently, aware of Terence's presence behind him. It was the kind of smile that you can't help but melt at seeing, the kind of smile that gets you out of trouble.

'So,' Terence said lightly, 'are you feeling better?'

'Listen, I'm sorry about that. I shouldn't've drunk so much and, yeah, won't be hanging out with that guy again.'

'Where were you?' By reaching for a fortune cookie at the same time, Terence tried to make this come off without sounding accusatory.

'Well, it was a mix-up. I thought we were just going to hang out at this—' He cleared his throat. '—public park. But anyway, like I said, never again.'

'Huh,' Terence said in a clinical voice, helping himself to another fortune cookie. Baffled by the change in Milo's mood, he cracked open the cookie and snickered. 'Who comes up with this stuff?'

Aloud, Milo read it: 'A dubious friend may be an enemy in disguise.'

X.

A week passed without incident, enough time that Terence felt comfortable in thinking it had all been a fluke, early teething days of a new relationship and a new place. They'd not had sex since, but the previous two times had been so awkward, particularly the last one, that Milo's reluctance was understandable. But for his part, Terence was becoming more accustomed to this new life abroad. After the holiday-like euphoria of the first weeks, followed by the unpredictability and newness of the week prior, it felt like a routine might set in.

It was all very different from the patterns he'd established in London, where everything was more or less 'as you please.' Here, every plan had to be thought through, coordinated, and scheduled around strict opening and closing times, WiFi availability, and space concerns. Those had never been considerations in London, a city that never sleeps. In Vienna, time was measured strictly by the clock, and all activities had to accommodate its tick-tock. You were free to meander, but only between certain hours. But this pushed Terence toward structure, and soon he began a routine of writing at home for two hours every morning, breaking for a lunch of sandwiches he'd prepare for himself to save money, and then an afternoon out either working from a coffee shop, doing laundry at the coin-operated laundry down the road, or grocery shopping before the markets closed at six. All of this meant that the things he'd found almost indispensable in his old life were no longer essential. He rarely picked up his iPhone, sometimes even forgetting it at home; he began borrowing books from the small *englische Bücher* section at the community library; and streaming on his laptop replaced TV. In this blameless quiet, he produced words he was proud of, and the novel he'd struggled to pick up again started to take shape.

'I want you to tell me more about your past,' Terence said to Milo after a dinner of microwaved meals that Thursday. 'Have you ever loved before?'

Earlier that day Terence had been on a tram, ambling around the ring road circling Vienna's city centre. It was past sunset, and the sky was that hazy grey of the late afternoon in early winter after the clocks have gone back an hour. He'd been working all day and then riding the tram aimlessly. This helped him to decompress after a day spent inside the minds of make-believe characters. That's when it occurred to him that he had always presumed to know, by circumstance or conjecture, Milo's innocence in matters of the heart. This, he reckoned, accounted for Milo's timidity and awkwardness.

'Excuse me,' Milo said presently. He stood up from the kitchen table and went to the loo.

I've gone too far, Terence thought. *Pushed him again, and for what? Does it really matter?* He tried to imagine Milo sneaking off to clandestine hook-ups with nameless boys, but the picture wouldn't form. Then, he thought of Jasmine Evans, and suddenly he felt sick to his stomach. By the time Milo returned,

Terence was ready to quash the whole thing, sorry he'd ever brought it up.

'Do you really want to know?' Milo asked.

'Yes,' Terence said, with more reluctance.

And as though to entrap him, Milo moved his chair closer, snuggling near to Terence in the already-tight kitchen. 'I met him at the hostel,' he said.

'And did you love him?'

'I don't know; I guess so. He was my first.'

'Your first ever?'

'First kiss. You were my first otherwise. Daniel was older than me. Five years at least. He liked to cook, and smoke, and tell stories. We went to the funfair last summer.'

'What happened to him?'

'He was a backpacker. He moved on.'

'And then?'

'I tried to stop thinking about him. He'd given me some advice, which I ignored, at the time, anyway. And now, he's gone. He's from America, so I'll probably never see him again. Been trying to find him on Facebook, though.'

Terence fell quiet. It scared him to ask what would happen if Milo ever saw Daniel again.

Something in Milo could sense the man's fear. He stood and took a step to the kettle, filling it with water from the tap. 'It doesn't matter,' he said. 'I'm happy to be here. With you.'

They drank their teas in silence until Milo spoke again. 'I miss your touch,' he said.

XI.

The days that followed were solitary and surreal. Leaves fell from the trees, rain poured nonstop, and the hours of light were few and far between. All of this contributed to Terence's growing depression. It had set in after their third time, though not immediately after. Unlike the other times in bed, there was no awkwardness. Milo seemed warm and satisfied afterwards as he cuddled with Terence and kissed him on the forehead.

But the next morning the coldness set in. It was as though the novelty of it had worn off, and the quiet nature of the place in which Milo found himself became clear. It manifested through the smallest of actions: the grumbled good morning, the one-word responses, his disappearance for hours on end ('studying,' he claimed). Terence thought Milo was just ill, a cold perhaps, or homesick. But there were no signs—no cough or sniffles, and for what home could he be longing? Terence knew better. This was avoidance.

Nothing is lonelier or more disconcerting than un-requited love. But Terence was truthfully unsure of what to make of all of it. He only knew that they could not carry on this way for long. He had to find a way to speak to Milo about it and to establish some ground rules, some mutual understanding of what it was they were doing. Terence thought then, not for the first time, of Milo's age and wondered if any amount of talk-ing could bridge that gap.

In some respects, it was as if nothing had happened. Milo went to his German class, Terence did his writing, and they pretended for and to one another that things were all right, or at least on their way to being so. The routine held things together like a point of reference they clung to with the grit of an addict. Terence con-vinced himself, by ignoring his heart, that this was all in some respects a charade for Milo's benefit, a stable home environment until they could smooth things over. But Terence did not, could not, grasp how dis-turbed Milo really was. Not until things came to a head.

XII.

They were spending the Sunday at home. Terence's idea had been to visit *Der Blaue Reiter* exhibition at the Albertina, but Milo's mood was so jolly the first half of the day that Terence decided not to risk disturbing it with the stress of a crowded museum or the idiosyncrasy of train rides. So, aside from the slightly perceptible temperament present in all their interactions, the day was going smoothly, and they were both in good moods over a spaghetti lunch and a Netflix binge. At about 2:30, Terence decided to nap. He'd left Milo drinking a Diet Coke and watching some inane reality TV show. To all appearances, his old self.

Terence awoke to a loud, unintelligible commotion in the living room. The bedroom was dark; it was after 4:30 already. At first, he ignored the sounds as a dream or as Milo watching the television a little too excitedly. Then, the ruckus grew louder. Milo's words became more coherent. Terence closed his eyes and drifted off again. A few moments later, he felt a presence hovering over him, but he hadn't heard the door open. Sitting up in bed, he switched on a lamp.

'You don't give a fuck, do you?' Milo screamed, his face a yellow piss colour. He picked up a pillow and threw it across the room with a surprising amount of force. It hit the dresser in the corner and a picture frame fell to the hardwood floor and shattered. 'You just want to fuck me and use me and treat me like a toy.'

'What are you talking about?' Terence was shocked, shivering with cold and a heartbeat amped up to maximum. He reached out to grab Milo by the forearm. His body felt hard and wet.

'Don't touch me!' he shrieked.

The door slammed.

'Go ahead,' came the shout from the other room, piercing the walls. 'Try and stop me from going, you fucking fag. You make me sick, bloody shirt-lifter—'

XIII.

Terence watched from the bay window as the horizon sunk into the recesses of the sky. Like the disappearing sun, he felt cast away in an impressionistic likeness of the world he'd known. Milo's erratic behaviour puzzled Terence as much as it worried him. Milo had been generally calm before; used-up, perhaps, but calm. And then, even when his mouth opened with the floodgates of hell, still his intelligent eyes held a sad, reserved naïveté.

Just as the last inch of sun was about to recede and leave the sky in cotton candy aftermath, Terence heard soft footsteps in the hall. A moment later, the front door opened.

Milo entered the living room and stood sheepishly, his mouth incapable of moving.

'What was all that about?'

Milo pulled at the ends of his jumper. 'What do you think?' he said blankly, though he meant to be snarky.

'I don't know. I was sleeping and you—well, I must've done something to set you off?'

But it was Johnny that Milo had been thinking of. Johnny, who he had loved and had been like a father or an older brother to him. Johnny who he'd always *wanted* to remember, even to Daniel, as a benevolent figure. But something on the TV had pierced his hippocampus; the memory returned with the forcefulness of boiling water.

'Just one last time,' Johnny had said. He'd driven Milo home after they'd visited Tereza in hospital.

'Don't wanna,' Milo protested, still visibly shaken from seeing his mother connected to tubes and fitted with restraints.

'Just go into the study and wait. Got a surprise for you,' Johnny said, in a voice so reassuring that Milo, at eleven years old, was convinced it would be different this time.

But it wasn't. And Johnny was gone soon after that, never to be seen again.

Terence is no different than that monster, Milo had convinced himself, so worked up in the remembering.

'Do you have paracetamol?' Milo asked, returning to the present time. His face grew pale and his voice shook with fear.

'What's wrong?' Terence asked.

'Like you'd care.' At once his voice settled into something ominous. Milo waved his hands, casting out Terence's attempts at comfort. Despite knowing better, Milo was unprepared to separate Terence from Johnny. Puff-eyed, older, comfort-facade men. He remembered the truth now. He could feel the abuse even though it had occurred years before.

Outside the bay window, the night air sat deathly still. The sky's splay of pastels turned to a deep purple. Inside, the tension threatened to burst through the silence.

Terence went to the bedroom. He came back a moment later with two white tablets in hand. 'Here,' he said, giving them to Milo. 'Paracetamol.'

Milo took the pills and swallowed them without water.

Then, to his own surprise as much as to Terence's, Milo threw himself on the sofa. 'Fuck you,' he said. 'Fuck this whole country.'

Terence waited, keyed up and speechless. He only blinked, did not move, and was about to speak when Milo sounded off again.

'Fuckin' child molester!'

The tips of Terence's fingers moved faster than the synapses in his brain shouting at him to stop. It was too late. His palm hit Milo's cheek. The smack knocked the boy backwards.

XIV.

Terence Matthews found himself in the McDonald's again, staring out once more at the club across the road. He tried to force himself to focus on the curious people entering and leaving rather than on reliving the incident with Milo and the trouble waiting for him at home.

As he finished his food, Terence felt an overwhelming need for a drink. He'd not had this desire for a long time, never being one to rely on spirits to numb his emotions or to get through circumstance. He imagined this was how it felt for alcoholics, compulsion driving him to the bar. He wiped his face and walked across the street. Inside, lights smaller than Christmas bulbs hung from every surface. He felt as dark and dreamlike as the bar. After a double, he left, feeling worse than before.

At home, the light that always burned in the hallway gave the place an eerie alertness. Terence locked the door behind him, hung his coat on a peg, and quietly stepped down the entry hall, unsure if Milo was in and not wishing to cause a stir. On a console table, he tossed his key and stopped to look at the things placed there: museum passes, sunglasses, a pair of leather gloves, his phone charger, and a recent edition of The Guardian Weekly. Where was Milo in any of this? Above the console, a circular mirror reflected the fervid light. *My god*, Terence thought, looking in the mirror. He stood for a moment and listened. There was nothing, not even the gentle up-and-down of Milo's snore. He'd not come home.

Terence picked up the newspaper and walked to the sofa, but not before peeking into the bedroom to assure himself he was alone. A little drunk from the double on the rocks, it took a moment for the tiny print on the pages to coalesce into intelligible sentences. 'Prime Minister faces leadership challenge.'

Terence sat upright. His mind fog cleared as he read:

Prime Minister Jasmine Evans will next week face a vote of no confidence in a motion to be tabled by the Opposition unless she can assure members of Parliament that her personal life and outside interests will not continue to impact her premiership. This comes after it was revealed that the thinly veiled accusations in this summer's bestselling novel *Noon at the Louvre* were, in fact, largely inspired by true events, if not outright fact-based. An anonymous source, rated by us as highly credible, has come forth to confirm Evans carried on a lengthy affair with an unnamed French citizen whilst she and her husband, communications expert Jon Evans, were living in Paris. While the relationship is said to have ended, the concern now is Evans's apparent attempts to cover up the affair and lie about the matter when asked about it during Prime Minister's Questions as recently as last week. According to The Times, Evans also threatened legal action against Terence Matthews, the author of the aforementioned novel, though the status of that claim remains unclear, with court records showing nothing has been filed to date. Meanwhile, the Opposition Leader angrily accused Evans of treating Parliament in a 'totally and utterly unacceptable way' and pressed her to tell the full story for the 'moral sake' of the nation. According to one poll, at least one-third of her own party are likely to vote in favour of passing a no confidence motion, potentially throwing the U.K. into a general election just months after Evans rose to power.

XV.

A thing, once remembered, can never be forgotten.

Milo came to learn this in those solitary days. He could not, would not, stay with Terence, so he took up temporary residence at the home of Dr and Mrs Hollinghurst, the parents of Tobias.

It came about by chance. There was nowhere to go. He had no mobile on which to ring someone, and even if he hadn't lost his phone at the factory building, who would he call? The only thing to do was to go the German school. There were drop-in classes every hour on the hour until 9:00 p.m. He planned to loiter in the waiting room's warmth until he could think of something. But Tobias was there. Shady, drug-pusher Tobias.

'Yo, Milo, where you been, man? You ran out the trap so fast the other night.'

Not that Tobias seemed to mind, but his voice carried. This was a particular quality Milo noticed in upper-middle-class boys unafraid of getting caught.

'I got issues at home,' Milo said. He knew that Tobias must assume he lived with his parents, but they'd never spoke of it, the extent of their conversation either the recitation of German phrases or petty small talk: the weather, life 'back home,' American versus European football.

'Yeah, I figured that when you punched me. You need a serious chill pill, dude.'

'Yeah, well, sorry about that. Nerves got the best of me.'

'What "issues" you got, anyway?' Tobias's expression spoke of genuine interest.

Milo's mind raced as fast as a Formula One car.

Intention is everything, thought Tobias Hollinghurst. He suspected that Milo wanted things and craved experiences he didn't yet realise. They were things Tobias wanted too. So, Tobias made him a simple offer: 'You need someplace to crash?'

The proposal came surreptitiously and with no obvious strings attached. This gave Milo pause. Tobias was at least partly responsible for Milo's troubles, and yet, here he was offering to bail him out.

'You can stay with us a night or two,' Tobias leaned in. 'Sure my 'rents won't mind if you crash. It'll be like a sleepover.' He looked giddy, a schoolchild arranging his first slumber party.

The Hollinghurst house, inlaid with gilt and glamour, made Milo see his own life as stale and colourless. For Milo, the world was an empty place. But for the Hollinghursts, life provided fulfilment. They could enjoy even the simplest things because the simple things they possessed were so much better than everyone else's simple things. They opened bottles of Burgundy at dinner with corkscrews coated in gold and topped in diamanté; they drank from stemless wine glasses of black crystal; they slept on sheets of pure white, as though they'd just come new out of the package. It baffled Milo why a kid from a family this well-off would want to spend any amount of time at a trap house.

A night passed. Then another. And then, Mrs Hollinghurst had questions. 'Who are your parents, dear?' and 'What do you plan on doing for a living?' Milo tried explaining that he lived on his own 'with a friend' and was focussing on learning German now. And maybe, he'd study art. Did she know Munch?

By the third day, it was clear he'd have to return to Terence. Tobias's floor was fine for a night or two, but Milo had no intention of gaining a second mother in Mrs Hollinghurst. He knew intimately the reality of hands-off parenting; the alternative helicopter mothering was not appealing.

XVI.

Almost seventy-two hours passed. To Terence, this felt symbolic. Either Milo would appear soon, like Jesus Christ rising from the dead on the third day, or that was it. He'd be gone for good and then—well, Terence had not thought that far ahead. Instead, his mind was consumed with the act of construction. He attempted to put together the pieces of their relationship, to define it for himself so that when Milo came back, Terence would be the wiser of the two, the self-designated alpha.

At the same time, though, a calm came over him like he hadn't known in many months. It stemmed from the news that Jasmine could soon be out of office. There'd been no word on the defamation suit. And though his letters to Jean-Pierre had gone unanswered, it seemed that the matter might resolve itself. If Jasmine were no longer PM, her claim would lose serious standing in arbitration, if she proceeded with the lawsuit at all. If anything, she might wish to stay out of the public eye following an embarrassing defeat. It was funny, thought Terence, how your life can suddenly improve in one way while the rest of it is an utter mess.

Within a few hours, Milo returned.

When Terence heard the jingle of keys in the lock, he bolted to the door. The jaundiced hall lighting was less ominous with Milo standing there, vague desperation painted on his face.

'Are you all right?' Terence asked as soon as he saw Milo.

'Fine enough.'

'Those things you said—'

'Sorry about that.' Milo said it curtly. He felt this was turning into a cycle: he mouths off, Terence gets angry, he leaves, they apologise. And they move on? 'And you, are you sorry for hitting me?' He hadn't meant to be so blunt. It was a reflex more than a thought.

They moved to the living room and Terence, uneasy, sat back on the sofa where he'd spent the morning thinking things over. 'It was a gut reaction,' he said.

Milo hovered overhead. 'And?'

'Yes, I'm sorry it happened.' This was the closest Terence could bring himself to an apology. It was the first time he could remember getting physical with another person since an unfortunate pub brawl back in his university days. He didn't think of himself as a violent person, but he was unaccustomed to insults on that level, especially from someone he cared for, perhaps even loved. There was nothing to do then, but to move on and pretend it had never happened.

Terence reached behind a cushion and pulled out a paper bag.

'What's this?'

'A new mobile. To replace the one you lost.'

Milo wriggled around the sofa, struggling with the resilience necessary to accept the gift and, at the same time, he thought that not accepting it would be tantamount to and as dangerous as consuming too much alcohol. Finally, he took the paper bag from Terence, opened the phone box, and turned on the device. It was a much nicer phone to the bog-standard one he'd lost, and Milo let a wave of gratitude wash over him but only momentarily.

'What are you doing?' Terence asked. Milo had spent the last few minutes with his face glued to the screen.

'Setting up Facebook.' The reply came without physical acknowledgement, no eye or head movement.

'How about that Christmas party?' Terence said to change the subject.

Something reticent in Terence's face left Milo flustered and on edge. Did he want to touch his man again or run away from him?

'Well, what about it?'

'Shall we go to the party? I can talk to Dagmar, get the details.'

Milo leaned over the sofa as if he was about to lower his voice to say something important. But he changed his mind. He reached over and kissed Terence.

NINE

I.

In a hotel room in Paris, Jean-Pierre put on his best white button-up shirt. Dior Homme with a Mandarin-style collar. He carefully laid out cufflinks on the bureau. Picking them up, he studied the face of Louis XIV emblazoned on the silver and remembered something the Sun King had once said. *Je suis en train de mourir, mais l'Etat reste.* I am dying, but the state remains.

He smiled, not as one smiles at a joke but with the knowledge of a forlorn truth.

'What's funny?' Jasmine asked.

'It's nothing.'

'J.P., come now. I know you.'

Do you? He wondered. 'It's only that we'll never see each other again.'

'Don't be daft, dear, of course we will.'

They were getting ready for dinner. They'd come over on the Eurostar last night, on the same train but in different cars. They'd booked two hotel rooms, though they'd only be using the one. They planned to eat in the hotel's private dining room behind its Michelin-starred East Asian restaurant.

This was all for her. Jean-Pierre no longer cared. He was ready to put the whole thing behind them. He'd only come here to tell her that, he'd convinced himself. He would tell her at dinner or perhaps afterwards in their room. Why had she insisted on seeing him, anyway? The affair itself, begun here in Paris with those not-so secret rendezvous at the Louvre, was over years ago, and yet here they were at the hotel to which they'd often snuck off. Neutral ground, she'd called it. A joke really since both of them had lived within walking distance. She in Alma-Marceau and he in Iéna. Lunch by the Louvre, sex in the hotel. Hadn't they been asking for trouble?

'I was wondering,' he said presently, 'why you asked me here.'

'And I was wondering why you came.' She slipped on a set of emerald earrings.

'So, it was a test?' said J.P. 'You ought to be furious with me, *non*? I betrayed you. What we had...'

'I was for a while,' she said, 'and then I thought, *What's it all for?*, darling. By the looks of it, I won't be prime minister by this time next week, and it will all have been for nothing. But as you say, our memories, what we had, were real.'

Jean-Pierre winced. 'You are a remarkable woman, Jasmine.'

For all his quirks, Jean-Pierre was easily satiated. No part of him, neither when the invitation came nor on the train ride over, had stopped to seriously consider why the woman he'd had an affair with, then sold-out at her husband's request, would be interested in reigniting their passion for 'old time's sake.' It was strange enough to think that he had somehow gotten away with the whole thing. By letting go of that notion of trying to discredit Terence Matthews and instead anonymously leaking to the press bits and pieces of the 'research' he'd shared with Tom, he became convinced that he could exist in the orbits of three people simultaneously without anyone noticing the connections. But you don't see the shape of the sun when you're glaring into it. You only get blinded.

Jasmine said she had to make a call and excused herself from the hotel room; she'd meet J.P. downstairs in the dining room. He was left there to stare into the mirror at the man he'd become. Though he looked nearly the same physically, he hardly recognised himself. The person he was now, in all the feigned glory of the role of cultural attaché, was a world apart from the young man who had courted the thirty-something English woman those years back. For all the stock he put in the role of macho male, he decidedly preferred the company of young boys and male servants to the glitz of five-star hotels and secret sex. This was something Terence Matthews understood instinctively. Suddenly, J.P. was chuffed he'd dropped his old friend a note just yesterday. After months of silent avoidance, he knew now he'd done the right thing.

Jasmine fumbled in her handbag for her mobile phone. It was the absolute worst time to be out of Whitehall, her advisors had warned. The optics of it alone would have it appear that the prime minster had given up. First, she had convinced Jon, and then her staff fell in line agreeing that a weekend away, alone, was precisely what she needed to strategise and find a way forward. Though privately she had little to no fight in her, she put on the warrior mask and promised to check in twice daily. She had lured Jean-Pierre to Paris with a single message. They would have one last secret rendezvous, a goodbye to end all goodbyes. Now, her plan was simple: A paparazzi photographer was waiting outside. Midway through dinner, she would ask J.P. to go out for cigarettes. The photographer would snap a photo and release it to the tabloids. Meanwhile, Jasmine's team had issued a statement saying she was in Paris alone considering her future in politics. The media would do the rest: assume that Jean-Pierre was the man she'd had the affair with, and that it was still going on. But Jasmine planned to deny the whole thing. She'd say that yes, there had once existed something between them, but it was over now; he just couldn't let it go. That would shut J.P. up once and for all. And so what if it ruined his reputation? He'd done enough to ruin it for himself. Hers would be only the final nail in his coffin.

She looked at her messages; only one from Jon saying there was nothing of consequence to report, and he was going to the cinema with an old mate. 'All good here, too,' she replied. Returning to the contacts list, she scrolled to the entry marked by a single X. She typed, her fingers moving fast as a bullet train:

Going to dinner now. To review the plan: In approx 90 mins, will tell him I want a fag and send him out. You photograph him leaving hotel—take from multiple angles, include hotel sign. I will take care of rest. Confirm, then delete message.

The acknowledgement came within seconds. She hit delete and returned to the contacts list, this time writing her public relations chief:

Confirm you've arranged the press release re: PM in Paris at XYZ Hotel considering her options.

Faking love was easy. Fooling her husband, for his own good, easier still. Coordinating this set-up had been more difficult. With these two messages, the logistics at last fell into place. If she played her cards right, the spin would come off: 'Crazy cultural attaché stalks former lover at Paris hotel, PM denies involvement and offers resignation to mend the nation.' A perfect way out. Not only would she save face, but she would leave on her own terms and exact revenge by framing Jean-Pierre at the same time.

II.

Awoken the next morning by a stream of radiant sunshine piercing the blinds, Terence, with his eyes still closed, felt around for Milo's body. He found the

boy under a mound of blankets, snoring in his characteristic way.

In the bathroom, the early dawn freshness was replaced by a series of small irritations. An awful smell
from the toilet in the adjoining water closet permeated
the walls. The bristles of his toothbrush had frayed,
and he'd only just noticed. The hair dryer was missing,
and his towel still had not dried on the rack from his
shower the day before. So, brushing his teeth with half-
effort, patting himself dry, leaving his hair wet, Terence dressed and went downstairs to see Dagmar.

Before this, his exchanges with the landlady were
mainly linked to the exchange of rent monies. He was
surprised, then, when she asked him in for coffee. 'It's
Brazilian,' she said. She always bought the same type
from Julius Meinl. Terence had heard of the upscale
grocer on the Graben, where everything was rumoured
to be two or three times the price of a normal market.
Dagmar, he realised, must have considerably more
wealth than her kitchen, no bigger or better fitted than
his own, suggested.

Dagmar seemed intent on making small talk. 'How
are you finding Vienna?'

'Fine, thank you.'

'And your work? A writer, no?'

Yes, yes, he nodded.

She spoke with the cadence of a lonely person. He knew that particular lilt of the voice.

'My Christmas party,' she said, saving him the awkwardness of bringing it up. 'I've been meaning to invite you to my Christmas party.'

'Milo mentioned it.'

'You simply must come. It will be here in my salon. Oh, you'll fit right in.'

They'd be happy to attend, Terence said, and asked if he could bring anything.

'Oh no, you've the wrong idea. I take care of *every*thing. Just show up.'

Terence smiled. It was refreshing to hear someone speak of salons and house parties and festive cheer. He liked this Dagmar much better than the crotchety old lady who had let him the apartment.

'There's one more thing,' she said on his way out. She fished through a pile of post on the kitchen table. 'A letter for you just arrived this morning. Here, saves me the trouble of bringing it up later.'

Terence looked down at the envelope. Return addressee: Mokrani.

Back in the flat, Milo was still asleep. Pleased to be alone, Terence tore open the envelope. A single sheet of parchment lay folded inside.

The bedroom door creaked open. Milo emerged. Terence shook his head, still looking incredulously at the letter. 'The French,' he said.

'Huh?'

He shook his head again. 'Oh, nothing, just the post.'

A very long pause. Milo looked at Terence. Terence stared at the letter, rereading it a second time. He was afraid to take the letter seriously nor to put too much weight on its promises. But what he feared more was spending his life riding the coattails of others. He'd begun to feel like a sell-out, though he knew the value of a feeling is only relative in the moment of contemplating it.

Milo bobbed his foot up and down impatiently.

'I spoke to Dagmar,' Terence said, folding the letter back into the envelope. 'I suppose we'll need to go shopping to get you something appropriate to wear.'

There was no discernible expression on Terence's face. Milo in his uneasiness waited for Terence to continue.

'We can go this afternoon.'

'Well,' said Milo, 'all right. See you later.'

'Sorry, come again?'

But Milo didn't answer; he was already headed to the shower.

The afternoon passed like a dream. For Milo, a happy one; he hadn't been shopping in years. For Terence, a hazy roar of mixed emotions. Jean-Pierre had written that he was 'the glue.' What did that mean?

Milo held up a navy blue blazer, the kind a schoolboy might wear. 'What do you think?'

Terence startled from his morose silence. 'Sorry?'

'Is this good?' Milo put the blazer on over his jumper.

Terence forced a smile. 'Yes, it's nice.' He glanced at his watch. 'Oh, it's getting late.'

'Do we have to rush?' Milo asked anxiously.

'Oh, uhm...' Terence's nostrils flared. He smiled again to disguise his irritation. He was in no mood for this, the simple tasks and pleasing others for the sake of it. 'Why don't I help you make a final selection,' he said, 'and we can grab dinner on the way back.'

Milo shuddered as if suddenly very cold and then pulled at the sleeves of his jumper. 'Last night I was so upset I couldn't really sleep,' he said.

'Oh,' Terence said, perturbed. 'You were sleeping fine this morning, though.'

'Well sure, after some time, I managed.'

Milo took in the grand expanse of the department store. His voice was anxious and his face, nightmarish.

The fight had upset Milo, that Terence knew. Still, why had Milo tried to bring it up now, when it was obvious that Terence couldn't properly respond? Feeling manipulated, Terence saw that on some level, Milo was pleased with the optics of the situation.

'I'll take the blazer,' Milo said.

Unbalanced, Terence stepped back, seeing real delight on Milo's face.

The plane cruised forward at nine hundred kilometres an hour. It was a short flight; they would arrive in less than two hours. Still, the two passengers in the second row of business class sipped champagne from miniature glasses and snacked on prepackaged canapés.

A flight attendant came round. Did the prime minister want a top-up?

'No,' Jasmine said. She looked giddy. As the stewardess turned to leave, Jasmine realised that her own smile was not one of apathy but of gratitude. It was nice to be recognised still, a week after her resignation.

She turned to her husband. 'Were doing this, aren't we?'

He nodded.

She'd asked as if they weren't already on the airplane en route. 'It'll be good for us, and not at all like last time.'

That it wouldn't be like last time was something they both wanted to believe.

'I just need some peace and quiet for a while; get back to us and how things used to be,' said Jon.

Extraordinary, she thought. The illusion of *that* couple—the pre-politics, pre-Paris, pre-child couple—

was so far from reality that she couldn't make herself imagine any semblance of it reemerging.

Jon seemed to sense her hesitation. 'Well anyway,' he continued, fiddling with his wedding ring, 'it will be good to start over again in a new place.'

He had said those words before. Jasmine leaned back in her seat and closed her eyes. She remembered a time even before the one her husband had in mind.

Jazz Shockley was sixteen and carrying her grandmother's letter in her front pocket. On the train ride from London, she had tried to hold it in her hands, but the weight of the paper—or, more precisely, the weight of the responsibility attached to it—had been too much to handle.

Entering the massive corridor, she'd pulled out the folded paper to check the room number. Her nan's penmanship was as precise as the directions she had written: 'First, go to level 0, Escalier Daru in the Denon wing.' Notwithstanding the perfect cursive letters, the words may as well have been written in a foreign language.

The massive, glass pyramid loomed overhead. A sign on the wall indicated she was on level -2. When she made her way to the Nike of Samothrace, the enormity of it took her breath away, and she fell in love with Paris then and forever.

Of course, she'd no idea then the role Paris and its famed Louvre would play in her life in the years to come. Would she have loved it so, she considered, had she known what was in store for her: that to get back to Paris she had to lose her baby? But, she remembered she *had* liked it with Jean-Pierre and not only because he was a distraction but because he was different. She would not have traded that, though she might easily have regretted her decision to ask him back again.

She had been afraid in the beginning that Jean-Pierre might choose to stop coming to meet her. She knew what she was in for but often wondered what he had to gain from it. There was a duality in his manner— now hot, now cold—that she first chocked up to nerves or age but realised, perhaps too late, that it was his personality, who he really was. And then when she and Jon moved back to England, she'd called it off. She believed her headstrong nature would keep him at bay. In rare moments of weakness, she sometimes thought of calling him, just to hear his voice or to relive for an instant the innocence of their affair. Yes, she always thought of it as innocent. Though she knew she was hurting Jon, she was helping him too by using the fling as a way to move on, to grieve. And then Jean-Pierre showed up in London. Nothing had happened. The sheer force of her will kept him away. At first. Until that book. She realised the power of words. Looking back on it, she ought to have known it was him all along, such was his nature—hot, cold.

But her revenge had not gone as planned. Though it had only taken that one text message to get Jean-Pierre back in Paris again, she would not have wished the unplanned consequence on him. Still, she couldn't help but think fate was on her side.

The pilot's voice loomed over the PA. 'Ladies and gentlemen, we will soon be arriving in Vienna. Cabin crew, prepare for landing.'

TEN

I.

The morning of the party, Katrin collected the post from the aluminium box in the building's foyer. Taking it to the apartment, she sorted through the envelopes, arranging the incoming mail into small piles to distribute to each flat. Ordinarily, when she was away at school, her mother would dispense with this task with eyes half-closed, such was the routine of it. Today though, Dagmar was dealing with florists and caterers and any other number of odd tasks Katrin knew nothing about, the tasks her mother had insisted on doing 'without help' for the last five years since the passing of, as far her daughter was concerned, the only love Dagmar had or would ever know. Katrin half-expected to see Dagmar flit into the room at any moment to tell

Katrin she was doing it all wrong. Letters should go on top of packages, sorted alphabetically and not by flat number, or some such arcane rule invented by women who need not work but do so for their 'health.'

There was an unusual amount of post, Katrin thought. Christmas cards and Amazon packages and plain white envelopes. After she'd sorted it all, there were two items left for Dagmar: a rectangular, scarlet red envelope with green lettering, no doubt a greeting card, and a rather large crate with slits cut into the wood at regular intervals. With no return address, the name of a floral delivery company marked the package.

Just then, and as expected, Katrin's mother rushed into the kitchen.

'Oh dear,' said Dagmar as she saw the box and before she knew what was in it. 'I suppose this means *she* won't be coming.'

'She?' Katrin detested her mother's way of speaking as though everyone could understand her interior dialogue.

'She's sent flowers to apologise, I suspect,' said Dagmar, getting a screwdriver from a nearby drawer, and sounding both disappointed and somewhat weary.

Inside, held in a glass vase etched with fleurs-de-lis, sat an arrangement of the brightest red roses and white heliotropes Katrin had ever seen.

'Whoever *she* is certainly spent a tidy sum on these.'

'Goodness!' Dagmar looked in the crate to see if there was a note. There wasn't. She turned her attention to the label. 'Oh, she flew it in overnight from a London florist.' There was a tiny note of relief in her voice.

'Oh,' said Katrin. 'So they're from the prime minister.'

'*Former* prime minister. And yes, I only hope it means she's still coming. Imagine sending flowers all the way from England when there are perfectly good florists in Vienna. But I suppose she doesn't know any of them here, and there's the trouble of finding one. And the language barrier. Oh, but she must have people for that, hasn't she?'

Katrin continued smiling, conscious that her mother required no response to this run of thoughts. 'And the card?' she said, holding up the scarlet envelope.

It was from an old colleague of Dagmar's husband who, she said, never failed to send a card and always failed to show up for the party. Inside the envelope was a two-hundred-euro gift certificate to Julius Meinl. It couldn't help but look small, even potentially worthless, beside the humongous floral arrangement. But Dagmar gazed at the plastic present with false modesty. Inside, she felt it was wonderful, even better than the flowers.

II.

Upstairs, Terence poured himself a glass of cheap chardonnay. In London, he might have popped open a bottle of bubbly on a day like this. In Vienna, he constantly reminded himself he was on a budget. At least until he could sell the rights to the next book, still unfinished. He looked out of the bay window in the living room and saw a delivery driver wheeling in large vats of beer and spirits. Now, he glanced to his right and made a face: half frown, half kiss. Terence glimpsed Milo dressing in the bedroom. A subtle bachelor sympathy had emerged between them in the preceding days. Terence had begun to realise what it meant to need someone. Thinking about it, a little tear formed in the corner of his eye. He wiped it away at once.

A minute later, Milo slipped on his new navy blazer.

'It looks good,' Terence said, calling from the living room. He felt generous and possessive all at once.

'Thanks,' Milo said, without looking away from the full-length mirror into which he stared.

'I'll get ready soon, too,' said Terence.

'Yeah, okay,' Milo said, with the canny little sigh of someone who has come out on top of a competition.

Terence muttered something. An unnerved, hesitant but controlled response, as though Milo's lack of words—or was it lack of gratitude?—cut him deeply. A thought came to him, one he had been trying to put out of his mind: Katrin, the blasted girl Milo had been so infatuated with was bound to be at the party. Terence suddenly wondered if isolation could be as fulfilling as companionship.

III.

Jasmine and Jon had been in their new flat for a week now, but the scale of it still impressed them. Jasmine stood in front of a framed print hung in the massive study. She was dressed in a solid navy dress, sleeveless, and a bit too provocative for a cold December night. *I'll cover myself with a scarf, she thought, or let my hair flow down around my shoulders like the woman in the painting.* She stared earnestly at the picture, hoping the name of the artist would come to her. It was a reproduction but a fine one. She could even make out the horizontal dabs of brushwork on the two main figures. The vertical lines of black paint in the background quivered. The picture sat in a plain birch frame.

'It's a Munch, isn't it?' said Jon, who had just entered the room dressed in his finest (and only) tuxedo.

'It's a nice one,' Jasmine said, remembering now that she'd seen the original in Gothenburg.

'*Love and Pain*,' said Jon. They stood shoulder-to-shoulder, emulating his idea of how couples should behave. This pleased him. As he'd hoped, a change of scenery was serving them well.

Jasmine considered the picture once more. A woman with long flame-red hair kisses a man on the neck as the couple embrace. 'More like a vampire.'

'Well, you're not wrong,' he said, grabbing her hand in his. 'It's been called *Vampire*, too. A man locked in a vampire's tortured embrace.' *And isn't that ironic?* he thought. He shook his head slowly and blinked to disguise his calculations.

Jasmine nodded, too, and said, 'How ghastly!' in delight but also in scorn of her own gleefulness. She let go of Jon's hand and reached for the cocktail she'd made herself a quarter of an hour ago but had since forgotten. All the ice had melted, and she frowned at seeing how watery it had become.

'I can make you another one,' Jon offered.

'No, no, it's fine. And you look very nice,' she said to change the subject. 'Oh, it's good to be going out as normal people. I've missed this. Getting dressed up, going to parties. No press, no pressure.'

Jon pulled a face, thinking about something else. 'Do you really think we ought to go? I mean with what happened and all—'

'I'll hear no more of it,' she snapped. It was a rare moment of raw anger. 'Besides, Dagmar knew nothing of *him*.'

IV.

An uneasy atmosphere invaded the flat in the hours before the party. Caterers took over the kitchen, setting up rows of aluminium trays and stacks on stacks of champagne flutes, kicking out Katrin in the process. Retreating to her bedroom at the back of the house, she walked through the vast foliage of the foyer, noticed the clusters of chairs in the dining room (*And where had the table gone?* she wondered.), and heard the squawks coming from the sound system being tested in one corner of the drawing room. It was a good job her mother invited the whole building to the party. *She had to; the noise complaints alone...*

The whole building. What had become of that boy, Milo? thought Katrin. Dagmar had said something about him asking after her. He was lonely, she supposed. A new city and no friends. She had felt that way, at first, in Switzerland. She would make it a point to speak with him tonight. Perhaps she could introduce him to one or two of the teens in the building.

About 5:30, Katrin slipped out for a walk. Or, rather, she had intended to slip out until her mother noticed and called after her to make sure she was back 'with plenty of time to dress and do your hair and makeup.' The gloom of the evening air hit Katrin as soon as she stepped out of the building. Haphazard little white flakes shot from the sky. Parka-coated children and their pea-coated minders hurried off in every direction for shelter. Everyone overreacted at this first sign of wintery precipitation.

She came to the gates of the Belvedere. The lights from the museum flickered like shooting stars punctured by snowflakes. She longed to go there and browse the galleries instead of heading back to organise herself for the Christmas soiree. She couldn't place her finger on it, but something sour and dyspeptic had come over her on the walk.

Back home, the building had a brilliant quietness to it, the calm before the storm. Still, Katrin couldn't shake the feeling that despite her mother's planning and the efforts of the caterers and the florists and the deejay and so on and so on, something was wrong.

V.

The front door slammed, and Dagmar went to look over the bannister. It was a day of incessant deliveries, and soon it would be an evening of incessant arrivals. 'Oh, come up, dear,' she said. It was Charlotte Hollinghurst, whom Dagmar had invited for the first time this year.

They spent ten minutes placing the elaborate bouquet in different locations around the flat, Dagmar holding it above a mantelpiece, over a console table, beside an imitation Doric column, while Mrs Hollinghurst pursed her lips and said, 'No, I think it would be better there...'. Charlotte was famed, at least among the ladies of the United Nations Spouses' Afternoon Tea Club, as an expert on all things home décor. Dagmar, a member of the group since its formation a decade prior when her husband was in service, felt that having the Hollinghursts could only improve the social cache of her annual Christmas party, but she also knew that women like Charlotte Hollinghurst were busybodies. Thus, Dagmar had invited Charlotte over half an hour early on the pretence of needing advice on where to place all the flowers and candles and accoutrements. In truth, the florist she'd used for the last five years had done the work that morning.

'You know I've been hosting this party for many, many years now,' Dagmar said with a little toot.

'Oh?' said Charlotte Hollinghurst. She tried not to sound or look annoyed, though it was clear Dagmar had very strong opinions on her long-standing event.

'Well, it is something of a tradition now, and we get a fair amount of interesting people. Have I told you we have a writer living in the building now? From England, in fact, dear.'

'Oh, do tell!'

'Terrence Matthews. He wrote that book about Paris–'

'About the prime minister's affair!' Charlotte exclaimed and gave a rather grim laugh.

'What? How's that?'

Mrs Hollinghurst, with the speed of a true gossip, explained the saga–as she knew it from the media–to Dagmar. 'Although there was never any real development,' she concluded. 'Nothing came of the allegations that Matthews actually knew anything or meant any harm.' She said this cautiously as though she had her own suspicions but was choosing to stick to the official account. A conspiracy theorist ashamed to admit her beliefs.

'Oh my god,' said Dagmar. 'I suppose it's good then that she's not coming.'

'I should say!' said Charlotte. 'But what glorious flowers!' She placed them above the fireplace and let out another awful little laugh.

VI.

Terence pointed at the door to Dagmar's flat. Painted a Christmas green, it elicited feelings of hot cocoa, Mariah Carey on the radio, and warm cookies. 'But it was grey just a few days ago,' he said. 'I'm sure of it. The same grey as ours.' This was their first real glimpse into the mania of Dagmar's holiday hysteria. Just then, a man dressed head-to-toe in black opened the door with a forced smile. A butler, Terence gathered, hired for the evening.

Never having made it past the kitchen that sat to the left of the entryway, neither Milo nor Terence had ima-gined how large Dagmar's home could be. The butler opened a second door in the anteroom, and from this vantage point, they could see her home occupied the entire floor. Standing in the crowded foyer, they could already take in the enormous drawing room beyond, at least the size of their bedroom and living room combined. It was 7:00, and already a dozen or more guests filled the flat even though dinner wouldn't be served until after eight. A row of three butlers of varying ages stood to one side with trays of champagne flutes.

Dagmar drifted into the foyer. An aura of outlandishness, semi-secrecy, and coyness enveloped her, and the black silk gown that hung from her short, plump body in just the right ways gave her the illusion of someone perfectly suited to both petiteness and width. The dress and her demeanour seemed to say that there was no way she'd trade her otherwise ordinary body for anything resembling the thin, chic silhouettes dotting the room. A whiff of Chanel and a string of pearls added to the allure. 'Darling!' she called to no one in particular. Everyone stopped and turned, hoping it was them.

Terence was the first to catch her eye. 'Hello, Dagmar,' he said, holding out his right hand.

She made her way to him, other guests moving to one side or the other to make room, some of them with looks of envy. She leaned in for a kiss. 'Terence Matthews, writer extraordinaire!' Her voice was louder than it needed to be. 'So glad you could make it!'

'Thank you so much for having us,' he said, a little embarrassed. Milo stood sheepishly behind. 'And you remember Milo, don't you?' Terence added.

'Of course, I do.' Dagmar turned to Milo: 'And Katrin is around here somewhere.'

For Christ's sake, Terence thought. It hadn't been five minutes and already, the girl.

'You know,' said Dagmar, leaning in and lowering her voice to below its normal volume, 'I just hate it when we have so many people in. So much work and so much effort to be "on" all the time, you understand.'

'Everything looks fantastic,' Terence replied, unsure if hers was false modesty or a glimpse of her true feelings.

'It's such a big day. My husband and I started these parties a decade ago when he was still alive and, well, just about everyone comes now. And you know, people can be so snooty about things that I feel this pressure to pull it all off perfectly.' She was rambling and at once stopped herself, as if suddenly self-conscious in remembering she was playing a different role tonight. 'Well, I don't know why I'm telling you all this, but I feel you understand, being a man of the arts and all.'

'I do. Isn't it awful?' said Terence absentmindedly.

'Oh, look, there's Susie.' A woman in a bright yellow cocktail dress waved from over by the champagne waiters. 'Well, ta-ta for now. Enjoy the night,' Dagmar said, already halfway across the room.

Terence imagined she'd be playing out the same conversation with Susie in just a moment's time. It was only 7:15, and already he needed another drink. He already longed for tomorrow morning, when the party would be over, and the enjoyable phase of remembering it, analysing it, and forgetting it could begin.

VII.

As she dashed up the road, Jasmine Evans frowned at the bits of dirt stuck to the soles of her pumps. She had imagined that Dagmar—this woman whom she had only met once through a friend of a colleague at the United Nations, one whom she could no longer remember—to live in a posh neighbourhood. Though Jasmine knew little of the city, she'd figured that Dagmar's rooms were similar to those she and Jon now lived in on the other side of Vienna. Then, she recalled hearing that Dagmar had inherited the entire building from her parents. Anyway, it made no difference now; they were late. Waiting on a cab had taken ages, and she cursed Jon for wanting to be like 'normal people' instead of pre-booking a chauffeur. Normal people take the Metro, she'd told him, so it would make no difference if they arrived in a taxi or in a limousine. When the cab driver had left them a block away, she cursed some more.

Inside, the party had already moved to the drawing room. She detested being late. No matter how stylish or urbane others presumed it to be, lateness was a quality she felt better reserved for those with no aspirations. And here she was, a first-time guest at a fabulous holiday party with no one but a humble butler to greet her and Jon at the door. They'd missed the cocktail hour and would look foolish hurrying to their chairs at the dinner table.

'It'll be fine,' said Jon.

They pranced into the foyer and then beyond to the drawing room, where a small group of finely dressed men gathered around the hostess. Jasmine circled through the room, smiling and visibly relieved that dinner had not yet been served. Two waiters came round with trays of small appetisers on wooden spoons. She declined and whispered to Jon to find them drinks. Jasmine locked eyes with Dagmar, and just for a moment everything was shining and suspended in time. Then, she saw him.

VIII.

Katrin found Milo in a corner with a drink in his hand, two or three steps behind that man with whom he lived. There was still a bit of time before dinner. This was one of her mother's tricks: to announce dinner would begin at 8:30 but then push it back 'out of courtesy.' 'Courtesy to whom?' Katrin had once asked. 'To those who arrive late by incident rather than choice?'

Katrin asked Milo to go outside with her. He agreed without a thought, without even the simple question 'Why?' that she'd expected.

She led him to the après tent in the back garden. They circled the squeaky squares of parquet and made small talk around the fire pit about how her family hosted this party year after year, how dull her schooling had become, how she was glad to be home for a couple of weeks. Like the tent, the conversation was a dreamlike extension of the flat. They fell into conversation so easily that Milo imagined it all to be some set-up or practical joke. No, she'd not asked him a singular question about himself. *And thank god,* he thought. *Let it be this way. Let her talk about herself forever.*

'I didn't even know we had a back garden,' he said when she finally took a breath.

'*We* don't,' she said. 'Only my mother has a key. She opens it up only once a year, for this party. Even I've rarely been back here.'

'It must be nice to be rich.' Milo found himself saying this among the lights and candles and smell of Christmas roses. Though he'd never set foot in one, he had the sense of being in a church. A boys' choir would sing at any moment.

'I wouldn't know,' Katrin said.

The lack of irony in her voice alarmed him. Did she take this all for granted?

She picked a rose from its vase and held it to the light, pretending perhaps to be interested in such things or to be less interested in this boy than she let on. 'Where did you study?'

And there it was: the questions about himself were beginning. 'Oh, here and there,' he said. 'Should we go in? I think dinner starts soon?' It was odd to be directing her like this at her own party, and yet he couldn't bear opening up to another soul. Not tonight, not to her.

They strolled across an improvised walkway lighted by metal-covered torches and wandered from the ante-room to the foyer. In a mirror, he lit up in shades of ultramarine and sapphire in his blazer and shiny new shoes. He and Katrin greeted unfamiliar faces in the drawing room, and across the way he saw Terence chatting with a man his own age. Instantly, spite rose in Milo. He turned to Katrin. 'Do you want a drink?'

'Yes, let's,' she said and led him off to a bar at one corner of the adjoining room.

Katrin ordered a whiskey soda. Milo uttered to the bartender, 'Same.' The faintly amber cocktail left sweet notes on his taste buds. This drink tasted nothing like the disgusting beer Daniel had bought him at the fun-fair.

'In here,' Katrin said. She pulled him by his free hand down a short, dark corridor. She pushed open a door and flicked a light switch. A child's bedroom came to life, all pinks and plush pillows, a white dust ruffle on the bed, and stuffed toys lining the shelves. 'My room,' she said in mock awareness.

Milo's mind began working overtime. A child's room, not unlike his own in the big house where he'd lived with his father and mother; just swap out the pink for blue. He had even had some of these same stuffed toys. The teddy bear looked familiar. Oh there, those troll babies with the orange hair. Was Katrin here so little of the time that they'd never redecorated? And he was here, in a girl's room. What was he doing in a girl's room? Would he even know *what* to do? He tightened his grip on the whiskey glass and took a swig. She motioned for him to sit next to her on the bed.

'What do you fancy?' she said.

He had no idea what she meant. From down the hall, he heard the doorbell ring and the flutter of guests. 'Huh?'

'Never mind,' she said, knowingly. She reached behind them, opened the drawer of a nightstand, and took out a plastic bag with a white substance in it. Using both her hands, she flattened out the bed comforter and poured out a small amount of the powder. She took Milo by the hand once more, stooped, and sniffed up the line.

Milo waited and watched. She pulled him down. He began inhaling through his nose, imagining this to be how it was done. 'Mmm, that's, uh, very nice,' he said, uncertain of the appropriate phrase.

'Oh, I got it off some local kid,' she said. 'American, I think.'

A moment later, Milo floated in rapturous surrender. It was all he could do not to kiss her and feel for his cock, as he would have done with Terence. But Terence would never, never be doing drugs. Milo thought of Daniel.

'Here, why don't you take the rest of this?' she said, handing him the bag. 'Looks like you need it, and I can always get more.'

But he couldn't, daren't. 'It's fine,' he said. 'You keep it.'

'Suit yourself,' said Katrin.

They returned to the dining room. Rows on rows of serving trays were placed around tables lining the perimeter of the space. At one end was a tall stack of white plates.

'Buffet style this year,' Katrin said. 'Mother said she couldn't be bothered to figure out a seating chart with so many decisive characters coming.'

The insinuation was lost on Milo.

'Do you want to find your, uh, what's he called? The guy you live with?'

'Terence,' he said. 'And no, let's stay together.'

She nodded. The coke trickle in her throat made her thirsty. 'I need another drink, anyway.'

The bartender prepared two more drinks. There was a commotion in the next room. Milo moved towards the door, still in too much of a haze to understand what the fuss was about. Nearby guests glanced at one another for assurance. At the far end of the drawing room, nearest the entrance to the foyer, stood a woman Milo recognised as the British prime minister from seeing her in the newspapers Terence left lying around. She appeared almost lifeless, barely moving.

Her gracious eyes could have outed Jasmine Evans with their hint of suppressed shame and hidden anxiety, but her posture was powerful; her stance more than made up for whatever awkwardness her pupils held. She did not dare lock her gaze with Terence. Instead, she looked ahead into the void of the flat, a very attractive apartment much grander and refined than she'd expected from the street. The shimmer of Christmas lights bounced off the unfortunate sequinned dresses of at least a third of the guests. Some had stopped to stare at her. Others whispered amongst themselves. She wondered if they were content to see her or embarrassed to be in her presence. The attention pleased her, and she resolved to make the most of it. Grabbing Jon's hand, she sashayed across the drawing room.

Dagmar was the first to see her. She batted her eyes twice to ensure it wasn't a mirage. A haphazard crowd assembled around the former prime minister and her husband, stopping them in the middle of the room to form an unplanned receiving line. This gave Dagmar time to think. Did she want this woman here? She had wanted the notoriety, the bragging rights to say she'd had a head of state at her Christmas party, but now that

Charlotte Hollinghurst had informed her of the circumstances, what with Terence Matthews, her tenant and her guest, being tied up however loosely in the whole matter of Evans's departure from No. 10 Downing Street, she wasn't so sure. But she could not ask the woman to leave. She had an invitation, for god's sake, and she'd sent those lovely flowers. Why? Why had she sent them if not as a rain-cheque?

In the centre of the room, calm began to be restored, though Dagmar saw Mrs Hollinghurst, of all people, dominating Jasmine Evans's personal space. The latter smiled humorously, as someone does when they can't bother to put on any other facial expression. Dagmar knew that look. She'd put it on a dozen or more times that night. Though Charlotte was holding Jasmine's hand in the way women sometimes do with one another—a feigned familiarity—it wasn't clear if Jasmine was trying to let go or if she had another reason to reach for her husband's arm.

Terence watched with sophisticated interest as she approached. What else could he do? He was stunned and turned into himself. He could not take the danger seriously.

Without warning, Dagmar was behind him, whispering in his ear. 'Use the loo if you need to, dear.'

So, she knew then; she was giving him a way out. 'Fine, I'm fine,' he said. He plastered a smile on his face so wide that it hurt.

The drawing room was large but not so large as to account for the unending minutes it took Jasmine and Jon to walk to where Terence stood. She looked beyond reproach, someone who could never have found herself caught up in an extramarital affair. He reminded himself that she had been, though. It was she, not he, who had done those things he'd written—however unknowingly—about. So why did *he* feel guilty? To add to the effect, her hair and make-up were perfect. He felt dowdy and unkempt in comparison. Her outfit, all too becoming, matched her immaculate white silk scarf. Terence peered at her chest so as not to make eye contact. An emerald necklace hung cleverly between her breasts. *She's beautiful*, he thought, and hated himself for thinking it. For once, he was glad he did not know where or with whom Milo had taken off.

With Jasmine in front of him now, he lifted his head, adjusted his smile, and felt her hazel eyes briefly but confidently focus on him before she seized the moment, as he imagined she always would, and spoke first. 'Terence! How wonderful to see you.'

X.

Jon had been standing behind her the whole time, both protecting and exhibiting Jasmine. From time to time, he cast satisfied glances at the other guests. His own pleasure derived from the fact that *he* was with her. It was an odd thing to love her so much, considering what she'd done and what she knew, all the things she'd never say. Of course, she had been with Jean-Pierre in Paris. How could he have believed otherwise? It was clear now, and he scolded himself for not knowing better on the one hand and not caring on the other.

Jasmine and Terence made small talk: the frightful Austrian weather; wasn't it funny they'd both come here to escape?

And yet, not so funny, thought Jon.

She was handling herself well, gracious under fire. Jon looked around again. As one of the few men wearing a tuxedo, he felt overdressed but also proud of himself for raising the standard. A dichotomy of emotions was all he was capable of this evening.

'Jon, darling,' he heard Jasmine saying as she moved away from Terence, 'you're very quiet.' She had the look of benevolence she sometimes gave him in moments when he wasn't living up to her expectations.

He paused, knowing it was reckless to venture into the territory he was about to force them all to enter, and yet, it was inevitable. 'Shall we talk about our mutual friend?'

XI.

Milo loved the way the drug removed his inhibitions. Or maybe it was the third whiskey soda that did it. He could see Terence across the room talking to the politician. He would have agreed to anything just then. So, Katrin saying, 'Let's go out back again,' felt natural, never mind the cold.

In the après tent, the candles glowed even brighter than before. The dazzling dance of silver tinsel caught his eye. Shadowy figures lurked in the corner, the silhouettes of a nativity scene or the outlines of occupied waiters. It was hard to know where to focus his attention. The faint roar of music from the drawing room echoed within the gossamer-thin tent walls.

Katrin put an arm around Milo's shoulders and asked if he was having a good time. There was another bar in the corner, set up for use later on, and she pulled him in that direction. Something caught his eye on the second or third step, someone else moving in the shadows of the canvas and plastic insulation. His street instincts kicked in, and he reached behind himself before realising he was carrying nothing to protect, no rucksack and no ill-gotten money. Tobias Hollinghurst appeared, looking perfectly normal, as if he had a key to the secret garden. He grinned and winked at Katrin.

'Hello there,' he said, holding out his hand. This was not the way Milo knew Tobias to behave, the boy whose affected street mannerisms were notorious.

Milo did not move, not even to take Tobias's hand. 'What are you doing here?'

'He's my friend,' Katrin said, a bit of cheer in her voice.

'Your dealer, you mean.'

'That too,' Tobias cut in.

Milo's eyes focussed. He noticed Tobias's immaculate black suit and stripped red tie.

'Just getting back to the party. Food's out, I think,' said Tobias.

Milo gradually took it all in, struggling with the connections. He realised the combination of coke and alcohol might not have been such a good idea. 'Yeah, okay, so you're here for the party?'

'With my 'rents. You remember them, ya?'

'Come up to my room later,' Katrin said. 'We can all hang out there.'

XII.

'You heard about Jean-Pierre, of course?' Jasmine asked.

'No?'

'Oh...' What Jasmine had to tell Terence made her feel apologetic. Jean-Pierre was dead. Apologetic because she knew he had liked J.P., and so had she. But she was also unnerved and for the same reasons. Yes, for those reasons and because she thought no one would ever know now of their liaison, or rather, no one other than Jon would know it was Jean-Pierre with whom she'd had the affair. This made her a little sad.

Terence did not act dismayed or particularly stricken. He did not move. 'Suicide?' he said.

'God no,' she said, 'an accident. Don't you read the papers?'

A deep frown crossed Terence's face. There was a time when he'd never missed a story. And now, he'd missed one very important one about his former best friend.

'It was in Paris. Jean-Pierre was leaving a hotel, after dinner, to get cigarettes. It was dark, of course, and as he went to cross the road, a boy on one of those electric motorcycles you see for hire all over town ran head first into J.P., knocking him unconscious on the pavement. The blood loss was too great; he died in hospital two days later.'

The first thing that struck Terence was the level of detail Jasmine possessed. She sounded so quickly resigned to the logistics, almost as detached as he had been unsurprised. He preferred her this way, though—controlled, matter-of-fact—rather than emotional or dramatic.

She, too, sensed a level of forced disengagement on his part. She remembered a grief training she'd been given early in her political career, a whole seminar on the grieving process, how news of death is perceived, and on coping mechanisms. She asked Terence why he'd said 'suicide.'

'That's just what came into my head.' He evaded the question. What had made him say it was guilt. Not his own, which would no doubt manifest in the wake of the news, but Jean-Pierre's guilt for having gotten Terence into the whole debacle, guilt for how J.P. had always been, at least since their university days. Hadn't all that guilt exploded into self-harm? That had been Terence's gut reaction: suicide.

Jasmine took his evasion as some sort of rebuke or even a hint that Terence knew more than he let on. Did he suspect the proximity of her to J.P.'s death or to his life? She'd learned, too late, the viper Jean-Pierre could be. Who was to say he hadn't played Terence as he'd played her and Jon?

'Will there be a funeral?' He would go, Terence decided then, to pay his respects. No matter the deceased's subversiveness, they had shared a camaraderie, and he had loved the man; he knew that.

'No. Apparently his family arranged a private cremation.'

Now Terence felt as though he might cry. The emotion bubbled all at once. He thought of the other people crowded into Dagmar's apartment with their drinks and canapés and plates of fried things from the buffet. He wondered what it would be like as part of their crowd rather than stuck in the individuality of his present circumstance.

Jasmine put a hand on Terence's shoulder. A shudder ran up his spine.

She felt the sparks in her fingertips. 'I want you to know that I'm forgetting the whole thing.' She stopped to look at him, expecting some signal of relief, some change in his face or manner.

He did not so much as blink.

Her next thought was: *At least I got to the photographer in time*. She had never hoped for Jean-Pierre to die. She remembered the commotion of the hotel staff. She'd ran outside like everyone else, never imagining she'd see his lifeless body on the road. And then she'd dashed back inside, shut herself in, and immediately called off the photographer and the press. Now, she had grown cold, as cold as she had become after Stephanie's death. But there was a difference this time: she saw the opportunity to put things right, if not with Jean-Pierre than with Terence.

'I know now that you didn't do any of this on purpose. You were the only one telling the truth all along,' she offered. The snap decision polarised Jasmine into the person she wanted to be—the 'let bygones be bygones,' new and forgiving person—and the cunning, manipulative person she had always been. But it was right to choose the high road, Jasmine knew. She wanted nothing more than to contract, minute by minute, into the microcosmic festivities of the night, the ritual and the mania, and then later to do the same, day by day, in this new existence that Vienna promised.

XIII.

Terence needed time to think. The loo was down the hall, Dagmar had said, though Terence was certain he must have gone the wrong way. This passage was very dark, and none of the first two doors he opened led to a toilet but were instead a laundry nook and what appeared to be a rarely used study. He heard noises from the next room. He took a cautious step and then another. The voices, one in particular, were familiar. Another step. The room's door, cracked open a handful of inches, let out a bright light piercing the darkness of the corridor. Terence lifted his hand, put it on the door, and prepared to push. Just then, the door pulled open the other way. There stood Milo. Inside the room, another boy no older than Milo lay shirtless on the floor; a young woman—he recognised her as that damned Katrin—in her bra and knickers was busy tidying-up the bedsheets.

With cat-like quickness, Terence jerked Milo into the moonless corridor and pulled shut the bedroom door. 'So?' he said, demanding an explanation.

Milo started down the corridor with pensive hesitation. He took only two or three steps before Terence latched onto his untucked white shirt, stopping him in his tracks.

'Where's your blazer?' It was the first thing to come to mind. His mouth turned down with a supple, spasmodic twitch.

Milo motioned in the room's direction, now dead silent.

Terence looked for guilt in the boy's ruddy face. He had glimpsed enough to know what had happened, a deck of cards falling before him. The three of them together; Milo's down-for-whatever attitude; all the license that went with never having experienced anything before Terence, before him.

'So, I guess it's not a secret,' Terence said, giving Milo a snide look, too tired for aggression. His voice plummeted a register, and the tone was empty of anything but regret. He remembered how he had once felt about families and cursed himself for letting Milo get this deep under his skin and into his bloodstream, and ultimately, into this heart.

The blur of coke wore off and provided Milo no reprieve. Terence might have been in the acceptance phase, but Milo was much further behind, in the phase with fantasies you never knew you had, where high spirits confront consequences. He smiled. Milo wanted it to appear conciliatory, pleading even. Instead, it read as defensive.

Neither of them knew what mattered now or what they ought to say. Neither could think straight.

Down in the drawing room, the music had softened, and folks were moving outside to the after party.

Terence found Jasmine in the après tent being chatted at by a frazzled employee of the United Nations. 'No, I think you deserved better,' the stranger was saying, casually brushing his sloppy hair out of his face.

'Well, if your first few months were anything to go by, you would have made an excellent leader.'

The man's hard-to-trace transatlantic accent gave little credence to his words, and Jasmine knew it. She yawned, not subtly, and called for Terence as soon as she spotted him.

'Seriously,' she said, turning to Terence while her would-be admirer droned on, 'one would think people could take a hint.'

He got it then. The man buried his head in his scarf and scampered off.

'Are you all fine, darling? You look rattled.'

Darling? It seemed they had turned a corner in their relationship. And where was Jon? 'Oh, I'm fine, I suppose,' said Terence. 'A, uh, just thinking about a friend that I came with, well—oh, never mind it.'

'I didn't realise you'd brought a date,' Jasmine said, disappointment fresh on her tongue.

'No, not a date... definitely not a date.'

'That's good news for me.'

The words startled Terence, but he let them pass, not knowing how to answer or counter them.

Her mind seemed to be racing.

His own thoughts were slow and unwieldy in comparison. He'd ordered Milo to return to their flat upstairs, but had he obeyed? Was he out cavorting again with Katrin or another boy or god-knows-who? And who was Terence to demand anything of anyone, anyway? And did it matter?

In a far corner of the tent, a half-dozen people assembled underneath a large television screen. At the press of a button, song lyrics appeared on the screen. A mirror-ball rotated from the dropped ceiling above the bar, lending even more intensity to the gold shadows of the interior.

'Do you sing?' Jasmine asked.

'Are you serious?'

'Sure.'

'Well, sometimes.' Dagmar's otherwise sophisticated party took a different path now, one Terence could not have expected.

Jasmine nodded somewhat as she appeared to ponder her next move. 'Sometimes,' she repeated.

'Yes, only sometimes.' Terence tried not to sound too smug nor too earnest to prove something.

'Let's go then.' She pulled at his suit jacket, and soon they were standing amidst the crowd of sombre but not sober karaoke singers. A Christmas carol flashed on the screen.

Before he could put the right spin to his words and make up some excuse for not wanting to join in, beyond the obvious explanation that was his burgeoning depression, Jasmine had already added her voice to the chorus. Her singing voice was soft and effuse, a voice Terence would never have guessed she possessed. He closed his eyes and let himself be carried away by the way she rolled her Rs on 'the weary world rejoices,' transfixed by her voice, by this person whom he thought he knew but now saw in a different light, and by his total failure to grasp how and where tonight was taking him. She reached 'fall on your knees,' and then her Os vaulted up to the ceiling and bounced off the translucent walls. His eyes locked shut, it was a moment so perfect and so dismal that he when he finally blinked, his pupils glossed wet.

'O night divine.' Jasmine smiled at what had become her back-up singers. The next song began, and she turned back to Terence. 'Well, I didn't hear much from you.' Her normal, almost snarky, voice returned.

A nod was all he could offer.

Jon appeared now, with three drinks balanced precariously in his hands. 'Saw you both from across the way. Thought you might like these.'

They took the cups and said 'cheers,' each for their own private reasons.

'Well,' began Jon, in the way that Milo had begun a hundred sentences, an observation not lost on Terence, 'it turns out that our boy is *shagging* his houseguest. Been holding out on telling us that much, eh, mate?' The way Jon said the slang made it sound as if he'd rather have used a more vulgar phrase but was holding back for comic effect.

'*No...!*' Jasmine's face lit up like a child's on Christmas morning. Suddenly her own indiscretions, which she'd been trying to atone for all night, showed themselves to be uninteresting.

Terence gripped his glass so tightly that he feared it might break at any moment, shards flying everywhere, piercing his palm jagged and bloody, exactly as he deserved.

'And that's not all. The boy's not over seventeen.' Jon slapped his wife on the shoulder playfully. No one seemed to notice that Terence had stopped responding.

'You tricky bastard,' Jasmine said to her husband. 'Who told you all this?'

'That old fart Dagmar; she's a hell of a gossip.'

'So that's where you've been?' said Jasmine.

'Yes. Can you believe it? Apparently, there's a Mrs Holling–something–Hollinghurst, maybe, whose son is in language school with Terence's toy boy. And earlier this Hollinghurst lady put two and two together.'

There was a long silence, signs of bewilderment at varying stages plastered on each of their faces.

'He's eighteen,' Terence said.

'How's that, mate?'

'Eighteen.' Terence looked up at the roof of the tent, took in all the lights and tinsel and foliage. When he blinked, a tear worked its way down his face. It was a tear for Milo, for Jean-Pierre, for himself, for his homesickness. A single tear encapsulating so much pain and loss and hope.

Jasmine held her own expression in place. 'Is it true, darling?'

Terence's head nodded mutely.

'I... oh, God, Terence... oh, I don't know what to say. Have you been incredibly lonely here? Is that why?' She took a step forward.

He nodded again. It was true; he had been lonely. It was exactly the reason. That and because Terence had felt sorry for Milo, wanted to take pity on him, a distraction from Terence's own problems.

Jasmine handed her drink to Jon. She took another step forward. 'You are not alone now.' She folded herself around him, as she might have taken a child into her comfort. 'We're here.'

A lovely sentiment, Terence thought. But how could he trust her?

Jasmine was not the imbecile others made her out to be. The mistake they all made—the press, her staff, Jean-Pierre, and even her husband—was the same mistake Terence was making now. She could see it in his eyes. They all wore disguises. And everyone knew it. There was the mask for work, the mask for friends, and the one for lovers. No one counted on Jasmine being the one person whose mask fell off the quickest. When she was absolutely herself, it frightened people, shocked them. Even at first with Jean-Pierre, she had wanted to tell Jon the whole thing and to reveal her lover's identity. She'd only kept quiet for *his* sanity, not her own. Other people, swamped in pretence, could not understand this simple truth. If Jasmine Evans said she'd do something or be there for someone, she intended to see it through.

ELEVEN

I.

Terence expected a fight, even wanted to demand one. There had been no time, though. Milo had packed his things and gone. He left behind the phone Terence had purchased for him and a note. 'Going back to my parents,' was all it said.

Terence never thought he was a man built for tragedies on this level. He knew himself as a person of frayed emotion, prone to too much reflection and not enough self-esteem. Expectation matched reality the first two days. He wept his tear ducts dry, imagined himself to be experiencing the most heinous form of heartbreak, and shut himself inside the flat with nothing except dusty paperbacks for company. And yet, after forty-eight hours, he had at last seen the futility of his behaviour. It was the best thing that could have happened, he assured himself. Now he knew who this Milo boy really was. And that might have been the end of it.

A week passed.

Christmas Day came, and with it, his return.

At first Milo was docile, almost jet-lagged, in a mild drug-like state.

He needs time, Terence thought. *And so do I.* But his next thought was: *I should throw him out on the street.*

Terence whiled away the hours alone, with take-out Chinese food like they used to have, Netflix binges, and too much wine. He asked no questions. He was afraid to. He feared they'd slip back into their early days when, but for forced pleasantries and sharing a bed, indifference and caution were the norm.

But then, the questions entered his head if not his mouth. Why had Milo not announced where he'd been? Where *had* he been? Had he come back because of Terence? Or to get away from something else? Terence wondered if he was prepared to continue trying to building a relationship, whatever that meant, with this boy. Or worse yet, to be a father to Milo. The events of the last months belonged to a lifetime ago. Terence would have liked to believe this.

Boxing Day. Would Milo like to go out for coffee and dessert? The pastry shop Terence liked was closed for the holidays. They passed the museums they'd once visited and stopped briefly in front of the pharmacy Terence had frequented to buy condoms and lube. A lifetime ago.

The city felt empty. The sky turned grey, and Milo was still distant.

Back home, Terence heard laughter in the hallway downstairs as they entered the building. He half-expected Milo to run that very minute to catch the sound of Katrin's voice fading in the distance, but the boy remained at Terence's side.

A while later, in the flat, Milo tapped Terence on the shoulder. Terence startled to be touched this way. 'Want to talk?' Milo said. He had on a jumper and trainers and seemed dressed to go out. He sat on the edge of the sofa, looking as uneasy as he had the first time they'd had sex.

'I might be getting married,' he said.

Terence felt all logic escape him. 'What?!'

'Well, it's been on and off for some time.'

'What's been on and off?'

'Well, my... my feelings, I guess.'

'What are you talking about, Milo? You've been gone a week. And now you're saying you've fallen in love in that time and are planning to get married?!'

'Do you mind?'

What a question, Terence thought. What was there to mind? None of it made sense. 'You're being silly.'

'Yeah, okay.' Milo looked down, studying the laces of his shoes.

'And?' Terence felt the sour cocktail of faded love and paternal care taking over. 'Who is it?' he demanded.

A race was on in Milo's mind to find words that would more effectively express something like the confusion he was feeling. People talk about the calm that can exist between two lovers, but this—the messy way things had developed with Daniel—was great, too. *Facebook. What a fantastic piece of work you are*, Milo thought. But Daniel was in the U.S., and he'd said he would wire Milo the money for a plane ticket tomorrow. So, one more night. That couldn't hurt.

'It's no one; never mind,' Milo said. 'Are you going to bed soon?'

Terence nodded. The foolishness of the whole conversation had left his mouth strangely dry.

'Okay, let's go,' Milo said.

'But I don't want to do anything,' Terence mumbled. The desperation in his voice faded in the room's stuffiness.

He studied Milo for a moment, taking in his frail physique, his underdeveloped limbs, and messy hair. He was a minuscule creature, Terence realised, and always had been. He looked on Milo as a hopeless child whom fate had put in his way to teach one or both of them a lesson. These maniacal attempts to make Terence jealous by suggesting Milo'd suddenly fallen in love or was about to get married only added to the effect.

'How long do you think you'll stay?' Terence said once they were in the bedroom lying under the blankets. He had resigned himself to the prospect of Milo leaving again. It had become a habit of his to disappear when life got tough.

Milo kissed Terence on the mouth, a forceful, waterless kiss. Terence recognised the taste at once. He'd never realised how much he'd liked it or how he'd missed it in those long days since Dagmar's party.

'I can't do this,' Milo said, suddenly springing up from under the bedcovers.

'I can,' Terence replied, but instantly regretted saying it. He could have seized Milo at that moment, held him down and kissed him without the boy having so much as a chance to fight back. But he wouldn't allow himself.

The next morning, Terence awoke early to prepare breakfast. He turned on the Nespresso machine and put two eggs in a pot on the hob to boil. Milo appeared in the kitchen some minutes later. Despite their odd conversation the night before, Terence didn't notice any change in Milo's mood. He did notice that Milo looked like he had been crying, but Terence decided not to say anything about it.

'How's your friend Katrin, and the boy—what's his name—the Hollinghurst boy?' He didn't know what made him say that, but Terence wanted to fade into the shadow of the early morning light as soon as the words left his mouth.

Milo's face was entirely blank, as if someone could come along and write any expression on it they'd like. He studied Terence for a moment.

The roll of water in the pot filled the otherwise silent space.

And all at once, Milo snapped. His features lit up like the colourful canvas of a Munch painting. He reached for the pot, lifted it off the stove, and held it high above Terence's head, standing on the tips of his toes for breadth.

Terence cried in fear. 'Oh. My. God.' He swung his right arm forward and hit the bottom of the metal pan. Scalding hot water flew around the room, splashing all over Milo's chest and arms and hands.

'Fuck you!' Milo screamed. 'Fucccckkk you.' He curled into a ball in the corner of the kitchen and wept.

By that afternoon, Milo was gone. This time, he left his key.

II.

Jasmine Evans kept her promise. On New Year's Eve, she appeared at Terence's door donned in white fur and red silk, a modern-day Mrs Claus fresh off her Christmas duties. He could feel his throat tightening. She'd come, she said, to ask him over for drinks. Just the three of them. Couldn't they be friends?

He stared at his champagne flute that evening, and for discrete and random seconds he forgot that Milo was gone, that Jasmine and Jon had once been the closest thing he'd ever known to real enemies, that Jean-Pierre Mokrani was dead. Ten. Nine. Eight. Seven. Six. Five. Four. Three. Two. One. Happy new year! A final drink, and he'd be on his way home.

Jasmine walked Terence to the door and waved goodbye. A flush the colour of purple and pink rose up in her, and she smiled. It was Stephanie. This was the first New Year's Eve in five years she hadn't spent crying into a bottle of champagne. There are such things as spirits, Jasmine believed. A memory, the unconscious flitter of emotion, the strength to make a new start with older people.

Terence's journey home was dominated by a ghost of his own making. He thought of Milo. What was that guy up to tonight? Where was he? And was he safe? To avoid entering his apartment building from the front and running into Dagmar, or worse, Katrin, Terence used the back stairwell. He opened the door to his flat, dropped his things on the entryway table, and threw himself on the cold, blanket-covered bed. Suddenly he was pleased to be home. He could have fallen asleep immediately and forgotten about the odd circumstances that had brought and kept him in Vienna. But in his exhaustion and in the spirit of new year's resolutions, Terence committed to taking out his laptop the next day to make a fresh start on his work. His eyes closed just as the thought manifested. He had never welcomed sleep so much in his life.

In the middle of the night, the phone rang.

'Terence, dear,' the voice said from the other line.

It took him a moment through his grogginess to realise it was Jasmine.

'We just wanted to say we had a lovely time tonight,' she said. 'Jon and I, well, we're just happy to put all the old behind us.'

What was he to say? They weren't quite in an 'it's never happened, just forget about it' kind of relationship. But then, no sooner had he heard her voice did he feel the drops of water rush down his cheeks.

From then on, it was Friday dinners and Sunday brunches, midweek teas and weekend trips. Terence settled into life in Austria as one settles into university: slowly, without much planning, and with the fresh thrill of every new experience. This became real to him after a weekend away in Carinthia with Jon and Jasmine. They drove there and back and returned to Vienna at two in the morning. Except for a few lively bars, the city was dead quiet. Jon took a wrong turn and, by mistake, they wound up circling Vienna's ring road. A few tourists mulled about for pictures. A handful of drunks and one or two prostitutes gathered in twos and threes. Jon parked the car and ran down the Kärtner Straße, leaving Jasmine and Terence alone. The first few minutes were a bittersweet silence.

And then, as if nothing untoward had ever happened, Jasmine pointed up the road to the Stephansdom Cathedral. 'It's beautiful, isn't it?' She began humming an old gospel song.

It took Terence a moment to recognise it. The words came to him: 'God will make a way where there seems to be no way.' A Sunday School teacher had taught him that song. It struck him like a lullaby now, a tiny bit of shared cultural reference.

Jon came back some minutes later, a McDonald's bag in hand.

The strains of the melancholic song stirred such nostalgia in Terence that he nearly choked on a French fry. He was reminded of life back in England, a life before all this. It was wrong to romanticise it though, he knew. Right before them, he again caught sight of the spires of the cathedral. He heard Jasmine's humming in his head. For a moment, he believed, perhaps for the first time, that everything would turn out fine.

III.

Terence heard of the wedding the following spring.

He was trying to get into the gym lifestyle. This was the Evans's idea, and they'd given him a gift membership. Standing outside the austere building with its concrete slab outer walls and revolving glass door covered in fingerprints, he felt like running away. This was ironic considering he had come there to use the treadmills inside. As he stilled himself and stepped over the threshold into the narrow entry hallway, his apprehension built. What did he know about lifting weights or flexing in the mirror or changing clothes in a locker room filled with muscle men who spent more time in gyms than they did in libraries? It had been a mistake to think he could join their ranks or even that he ought to. He only knew that men should spend time in gyms. Jon Evans had said as much. Wouldn't Terence like to 'bulk up a little' to get 'back on the market'?

Terence hurried into the locker room. With a speed that would rival a child unwrapping gifts on Christmas morning, Terence tore off his street clothes and threw on his workout kit. It was only after he had turned the numbers on the padlock that he realised the room was empty. He'd been in a rush for nothing.

The gym floor, however, was filled with what he imagined were the usual sort of gym-goers. Men looked at themselves in the mirror between every other set of free weights, sometimes flexing for added effect. Young women posed for selfies in mid-lift, while older women, who apparently only worked out in pairs, gossiped about their husbands and children as they did aerobics or peddled bicycles. The ironic part of it was that the folks who appeared the least suited to the gym —those few with beer bellies, fine lines and wrinkles— were the busiest. Moving up and down on the step machines, doing pull-ups and spin classes. Very little socialising. *These are my people*, he thought, making his way to the row of treadmills lining the north wall of the gym.

He had forgotten to bring his earphones, and concentrating on the TV screen on the machine was difficult. He began to make up names and stories for the people around the gym.

A certain familiarity developed as he made his way from level one to two and finally to seven in treadmill intensity. 'Christopher' is the instructor of the Pilates class taking place in the room just behind the treadmills, which Terence could see in the mirror's reflection just in front of the machines. Terence felt a bit of envy when he glimpsed Christopher's well-kept dreadlocks. What do the eight white women in the class make of their slight but very flexible teacher? Is he their sex object? Do they mind that he's black?

In the other corner on the gym floor, 'Mitchell' is punching a heavy bag, pretending to be Rocky or some kind of superhero, even though he looks to be pushing forty-five. On a stretching mat is 'Carlene,' a girl in her late teens who looks like she might have been friends with Milo if he'd had any friends apart from Katrin and that Hollinghurst boy. But Terence knew he wouldn't mess with this girl, this Carlene. She'd just done the splits, and the muscles protruding from her legs looked as though they could inflict serious damage. Nearby, a middle-aged man, whom he called 'Rex,' did push-ups. His salt-and-pepper hair caught the light just so. *Oh!* Terence thought, nearly tripping on the treadmill. It was no 'Rex,' but Jon Evans.

Back in the locker room, Terence spent an inordinate amount of time peeling off his shorts, T-shirt, and tube socks, all of them drenched in sufficient sweat. Jon accompanied him to the changing room, and Terence felt very conscious about Jon looking on, as though his eyes would judge the little bit of extra pudge on Terence's waistline or the smallness of his pectorals, even though they'd just come from the gym floor. It ought to have been a moment for praise or respect, considering that many, many people do nothing about their ageing bodies. But Terence felt only judgment. *You've not done enough. Until you look like the perfection of a porn star or a shirtless Instagram model, you have not done enough.*

Jon paid little attention to Terence. He scrolled through his Facebook, stopping now and then to like a photo or leave a comment. 'Look here,' he said, holding out his phone for Terence to see. 'There's an expat party tomorrow night. You want to go?'

'Who's that?' Terence said. The post above the one Jon was showing him caught his eye.

'Oh, uh, that's a friend of my nephew's.'

'Your nephew?'

'Yeah. My nephew studied in America, and this chap was his roommate there. The fella was in the UK last summer and my nephew asked Jazz and I take him to dinner. Nice enough guy.'

Terence grabbed the phone. 'That's his name? Daniel?'

'Yes...?'

'What else do you know about this Daniel?'

'Uhh, not much. He mentioned something about travelling around France after he left England.'

'In France? Paris?... Don't you recognise the other guy in the photo?'

Jon shook his head, unsure of the fuss.

'That's Milo. The boy—the lodger I had back in winter.'

'Christ!' Jon took back his mobile phone. Daniel had posted a single photo: he and Milo at a county courthouse in Ithaca, New York.

The blank months. If Terence were to divide his life into categories based on the people whose bed he'd shared, he'd divide it into those before Milo and those after. And it was incredibly stupid, he often thought, to think this way. Milo had been nothing more than a mistake, a boy who had seemed to throw Terence's life off course but had in fact made little difference.

There was an alternative universe into which Terence sometimes let himself venture. It was one in which Milo had stuck around, they'd worked through their problems, and they'd defied all odds to be 'that couple' that people envy. But then reality would intervene. Who were these people Terence so wanted to impress? And in what world did a child like Milo grow to be a man overnight?

The truth was that Milo lived somewhere else now and Terence lived in Austria, lonely and still alone. He filled the summer months with one-night stands and hook-ups and a date or two with might-be-if not-for men. The days passed, as they always did, with Milo or without.

Each encounter—with Jasmine, with Jon, with the sultry and nameless men who came and went—felt as though Terence were leaving his old self behind. By giving himself the freedom to move forward, he was reducing his hold on the past, but only in so much as his physical self would allow. His thoughts lingered sporadically and sometimes unconsciously on Milo. Terence hated himself for it, but there was nothing to do but let time heal him. Every life is unexplainable, he kept telling himself. No matter how many facts are revealed, no matter how many apologies were made, the essence of who we are remains hidden. None of it matters very much, though. He would publish his new novel and carry on living, just as he'd always done.

IV.

In late August, Dagmar called Terence, even though she could just as easily have talked to him in person. 'You'll never guess who is staying with us for a night, standing right in front of me now.' He had already guessed but pretended not to care. 'Well, he's just passing through you see by, umm, him*self.* He asked Katrin, ever so politely, if I'd mind if he bunked here for the night. And how could I refuse? He was such a good friend to Katrin, it seems to me, and well, I never understood why you two split, but oh, well–'.

Dagmar's knack for talking too much had not changed, Terence realised, though he'd kept his distance from her since that fateful Christmas party, preferring now to transfer his rent money rather than hand it to her in person.

'Anyway,' she went on, 'the fact that you refuse to guess says a great deal.'

Terence was quiet. He felt empty. Not sad, hurt, or angry; none of the emotions he'd expected to feel had surfaced.

'Well, won't you say anything?' Dagmar said. There was a rustling sound on the other end of the line.

Finally, Milo's voice came through. 'Tom,' he said.

Terence thought of Jean-Pierre. No one but the two of them could say his name that way. 'Milo,' he said, trying to force himself to sound casual but also to show he'd forgotten nothing.

Milo rambled on. He had a new flat in South London. And a job as a photojournalist. He was in touch with Katrin on social media, and that was how he'd kept in contact with Daniel. But Daniel was in prison now. Milo's parents were fine. And he was happy to call Arsenije his father now, he said, as the man had 'truly changed.' Milo gave Terence his number to use 'if you ever need it.' On and on. Terence only listened.

'Well, I'm learning to be happy,' Milo concluded.

'Good for you,' Terence said.

Epilogue

Halfway up New Bond Street, Milo opened the door of a coffee shop. Soft music played from a single speaker behind the till. A fat, jolly barista came to take his order. He sat down with his cappuccino and looked out the window. From here, he imagined seeing himself across the street crouching there with a felt top hat and a grubby rucksack, wearing the feigned look of someone desperate for something. And he could almost picture Terence, too. Almost.

Milo walked to the tube. Once home, he splashed his face with water, tore off his clothes, and lay in bed naked. Though it was summer, the room was cold and silent. He debated trying to fall asleep; fatigue sent a chill through his bones. A hint of jet lag pounced on him. *I should have stayed longer*, he thought. *Gone up to our—no,* his *flat. Tried speaking with him.* But then, Milo heard voices in the hall talking about a carnival in central London. *Could it be the* same *funfair*, he wondered? The voices rose, became indistinguishable, and he felt his courage running low. In panic, he tried to think of Terence instead of Daniel. But Milo's mind refused to survey that old flame or even to conjure him. He could dream up Tereza and Arsenije, whom he hoped—despite how he'd lied to Terence—was dead. And then, he thought of the moment, at the house in New York, when the police had shown up to take Daniel.

'What do you mean you did it?'

'I ran over that French guy. On my Vespa in Paris.'

'No, it's not true. If you did, they would've... would've come for you earlier. Tell me he was crossing where he shouldn't have been or it was someone else. It wasn't you. How could it have been you?'

But it had been Daniel. Milo's mind again attached meaning to the realisation. His brain lagged behind logic. He felt the pangs of sleep taking over.

His mobile phone rang.

'Hello?'

'Milo? It's Terence.'

Acknowledgements

My gratitude to Daniel Burger, Lali Sindi, Cheryl Stewart, Milena Usai, Jennifer Prince, and Jasmine Savage-Watts. Their encouragement and feedback made this an infinitely more readable novel.

I thank Bojan Kupirovic and the team at the American Library in Paris for the valuable research assistance. And thanks to my publicist, Cami Hensley.

My chaotic prose has benefitted from the work of an erudite editor. Thank you, Nancy Browning.

Most of all, I thank my husband. It's Lester who provides the means to make this all happen, and that's why every book I write is dedicated to him, as is my life.

Author's Note

LGBT people comprise up to 24 per cent of the youth homeless population in Britain. LGBT young people are often disproportionately likely to become or remain homeless due to overt discrimination. Organisations such as the National Coalition for Homelessness in the United States and *akt* (formerly The Albert Kennedy Trust) in the U.K. work to ensure people live in safer homes, free from fear. Please consider supporting one of these organisations.

A number of paintings by Edvard Munch are described in this novel. *Self-Portrait with Cigarette* (1895) is in the National Museum, Oslo. *Self-Portrait in Hell* (1903) is in the Munch Museum, Oslo. Six versions of *Love and Pain* (1893-95), also called *Vampire*, exist; three versions are at the Munch Museum in Oslo, one is at the Gothenburg Museum of Art, one is owned by a private collector, and the last one is unaccounted for.

Jeremy C Bradley-Silverio Donato
is the author of the bestselling novel
My Memory Told Me a Secret. He was named 2020
Writer of the Year by the IAOTP. He lives in Paris.

www.jeremycbradley.com

Please consider leaving a review of this book on Amazon, Goodreads, Barnes & Noble, and any other site of your choice. Reviews help independent authors get the recognition they deserve.

Also by Jeremy C Bradley-Silverio Donato:

My Memory Told Me a Secret
2019 Wishing Shelf Book Award Finalist
#1 Hot New Release

Set in the months before and after a 30-something discovers that his partner has infected him with HIV, Jeremy Bradley-Silverio Donato's debut novel explores the inexplicable feelings that accompany the disintegration of relationships and the connections between cultural memory and identity.

Virginia Woolf and The Judicial Imagination

Envisage courts of law integrating best judgement with the gift of imagination. What if our legal system could be administered from a place of connected empathy? Drawing on passages from the works of Woolf, the author argues for the inclusion of narrative within legal theory as a means to improve law's aims.